Affiliated II: Black Pablo

A novel by
Ra Jones

StreetLink Publishing

Affiliated II: Black Pablo

ISBN 13-digit 978-0692426852

ISBN 10-digit 069242685X

Edited by Mary McBeth, www.UrbanFictionEditor.com
Layout and Interior Design by: UrbanFictionMedia.com

Special Thanks

To all of my readers from the start and supporters from the heart: I love you all and wish you many blessings. I hope that you enjoy the second edition to the trilogy and would like to hear the feedback. Sorry for the wait, but it has arrived. Enjoy.

Prologue

Silence, that's all there was during the flight. We were on a private jet, and the men walked around, silently packing guns into the luggage. They looked like machines waiting for orders. I didn't want to say anything to them, but I needed to know where I was going. After hours in the air, I heard someone come over the radio saying that we were reaching Mexico.

"Mexico," I said to myself. All the while, I couldn't help but think about Shai and Moni. I wondered what had happened to Rell. I was sure I was on my way to my grave. Being taken away in the midst of all the commotion was starting to worry me. All the money wasn't worth this bullshit. But I love the dough, and I love the game. It was a rush. If El Chapo wanted me dead, then I would be by now. I would probably be laying next to T-Mac right now. This had to be something else.

The plane landed and fear shot through my mind. I was on Mexican soil, totally lost in unfamiliar territory. Nothing could be worse than that.

"Get up," the Mexican said, waving me towards the door. We landed in Mazatlan, Sinaloa, Mexico, where El Chapo lived. I exited the plane and walked down the steps. Two G55 Mercedes Benz trucks awaited. One of the Mexicans opened the doors, and we got inside. I sat in the back as the two guards in front spoke in

Spanish. They were talking about me. "The American looks dangerous. I wonder, is he as deadly as he looks." They laughed.

We traveled through hills and valleys until we reached El Chapo's residence, somewhere in the middle of the jungle. The gates opened, and we drove down a long dirt road, passing two other buildings before finally reaching the main house. It wasn't a mansion; it was much bigger, more like a castle.

"Hello, Señor Ty." I was greeted by a slim Mexican. "El Chapo is waiting for you." He waved for me to follow him, then whistled to the other men to stop standing around. They walked off quickly to secure other areas.

I was still unable to speak. I didn't know what was about to happen to me. At every turn, I prepared myself for the worst. I had never witnessed this type of shit firsthand. To be a regular little street hustler is one thing, but to be a drug lord is a whole 'nother level of the game.

I wasn't rehearsing shit in my head though. Whatever happened was going to happen. We walked through the courtyard outside of the home, over to a building that sat at the bottom of a hill. A couple of guards stood at the door as we walked up; they opened the door. The slim guy stepped behind me and held out his hand. "After you," he said.

I hesitated and one of the guards pushed me. I stepped in slowly. I was ready for whatever, even if it was a set up and I was clearly out-numbered, I still had to go down fighting. As I entered the room, I saw a tall big dude in the corner and a short stocky dude standing between him and a big hole in the wall. The hole was dark and about the size of a basketball.

"Tyrek?" El Chapo extended his hand. He was the short guy with the stocky build and looked to be about in his late forties, maybe early fifties. He had a mean demeanor about himself, and he looked dangerous. I shook his hand.

"You have created a problem for me, within my organization. A problem that I must exterminate." He paused looking at me. "See, I hate problems. And I hate rats." He stepped up close to me. He searched my face for an expression of guilt, but I wasn't giving any sign. I would never be a rat. He walked off and picked up a machete from the corner.

A door slammed somewhere on the other side of the wall.

"With rats, I wait patiently." El Chapo clutched the machete with two hands, as if he was getting ready to chop down a branch. "Patiently, until the rat sticks his head out the hole."

I heard scuffling and screaming on the other side of the wall, then a man's head was forced into the hole. El Chapo lifted the machete and swung down, chopping through the man's neck like butter. His head rolled down in front of me. I looked down at the face. I had seen him before, he was one of the guards at Elan's spot.

"I am still exterminating because of you," El Chapo said while flipping the machete out of his hands like it was just a table knife. He kicked the head out of his way, into the corner, as he walked up to me. "You created this problem, so why should I take care of your mess? I got rid of your problem, so you will get rid of mine." He walked past me and out the door. The big dude pointed for me to follow.

We walked back up the hill and into the house. A guard brought a towel to El Chapo and pulled a chair out from the table. He wiped his face and hands then sat down.

"I have a nephew in Chicago," El Chapo said as he fired up a cigar. "He has been a pain. Cost me millions. Since he is my sister's child, no one of Latino descent can kill him. So you will."

I nodded my head. I could tell this was a order, not an option. There was nothing I could say.

"In return, you will no longer deal with Meno, you will deal with me through Chavez. Kilos of cocaine, heroin, or tons of weed, it's your choice." He looked up at me after dumping his ashes. "Well?" he asked impatiently.

I was fed up with being forced into situations with these motherfuckers. I wanted to let him know how I felt, but saying the wrong thing would get me a trip down to the hole in the wall.

"Look, El Chapo, I'm saying this with the utmost respect, I'm not trying to get tied up in something I can't get out of," I said.

He started laughing, then the others began to laugh. "Señor, that is too late," he said. His face grew serious. "You will not and cannot leave, except through death. That is the only out." He leaned across the table. I looked at the guards, then at him.

"Believe me, Señor Ty, there are many benefits to Mafia Mexicana. You don't go to jail, and on some occasions, we kill rats and pay judges. You are among the elite of the under world now. And plus, if you fuck up, you don't die, just your family." He laughed. This motherfucker was crazy.

"That's funny?" I smiled.

"No! It's not funny." He grew serious again. "What is funny is you thinking this is a game. This is a business, and you have just become an executive. Deal with your position. Now, I will arrange two tons of mota and two hundred kilos: one hundred cocaine and one hundred heroin. Every month. Chavez will notify you for the money, and the shipments will be delivered by a diesel truck. The driver will park the rig at my warehouse in St. Louis. You will be responsible for unloading it and leaving the trailer secured. Payments will be two point five million a month, non-negotiable. By the time you get home, the first shipment will be there."

I tried to do the math on the numbers he threw out there. Damn, the deal was too sweet, I wouldn't fuck that up if I could. He waved his hands to one of the guards standing near.

"Take Señor Ty to Chavez, and tell him to see to it he has a good time."

* * *

Chavez walked me through the mansion, giving me a brief tour, then escorted me to the room that I would be staying in.

"If you need anything, just ask," Chavez said.

"Where's the phone?" I asked.

"Anything but that, no calls from here," Chavez said, leaving the room.

I lay down and put my hands behind my head. The room and balcony were elegantly decorated with silk drapes that floated from side to side as the breeze blew inside. I got up and stood on the balcony. From my room, I could see the building down the hill. I watched for a while. Gunshots sounded shortly after two guys walked inside. Then, the same two guys came out dragging bodies and tossed them aside. They looked like construction workers throwing trash out of a building. I walked back into the room and lay back down. I listened to the shooting for another hour or so before it stopped, then I drifted to sleep.

I woke to a cart being rolled into the room. An elderly woman set trays down on the table on the balcony. She nodded her head, then left the room. I got up and walked out to the table. I lifted the stainless steel covers from the plates. It was a Mexican steak dish called chuleton, a T-bone steak with Mexican spices, along with a bottle of Vueve Cliquet and a pitcher of water. I sat down and tried to eat the food. It was delicious, but I couldn't eat. I didn't have an appetite. I kept picturing Shai lying dead.

Chavez entered the room. "Señor, get ready, we go to have a drink," he said, sitting down at the table. He noticed I had barely touched the food. "Not much of an appetite?"

"I'm cool," I said.

He just looked at me curiously. "Let's take a ride," he said, getting up from the table.

* * *

Rell sat in the County Jail for three days. It took him that long to get in touch with his lawyer. He was charged with possession of a firearm and aiding and abetting a criminal. He wondered why Ty didn't come get him. He wondered why Moni wasn't answering her phone. He wondered what the fuck was going on, and he was on edge.

Others in the blocks kept bitching about him using the phones so much. Then one day, one of the dudes tried him. Rell snatched the receiver from the wall and almost beat the dude to death. If the dude wasn't such a asshole to the cops, they would have charged Rell with assault. They threw Rell into segregation for the time being.

He tried the lawyer every day until he finally reached him. By that time he was pissed. The lawyer was paid a fifty thousand dollar retainer fee up front for any trouble they might come across. So when Rell finally contacted him, he came quickly. Rell waited until they got out of the police station after the lawyer bonded him out, then he hit the lawyer in the stomach. Rell bent down to his ear.

"Listen, mafucka, I didn't pay you to fuck off while I sit in jail." Rell pushed him away by the face and walked to the car. "Hurry up and take me to get a rental."

* * *

Shai got up from the bed. She hated the smell of hospitals. She had been running to the bathroom all day, vomiting. She came back into the room, and Moni was sitting up in her chair. She had stitches on the side of her head.

"You hear anything yet?" Shai asked, hoping that Ty had called to see where they were. She sat down on the bed and grabbed the phone.

"Naw! The phone been dead, I just got a charger," Moni said turning over to her side. She had been thinking about Rell. She hadn't known how much she cared for him until now.

Shai dialed Meno; she needed to know what had happened.

Meno picked up, and Shai could hear some Mexicans talking in the background. She tried to make out what they were talking about, but couldn't.

"Meno?" she said, wondering if he was on the phone.

"Shai, what,—I mean—how are you doing?" Meno said, sounding surprised.

"What is going on?" Shai started to cry. "Ty is missing, and we can't find him at all!"

Meno wanted to tell Shai about Ty's whereabouts, but he couldn't. He couldn't tell Shai that Ty was now officially tied to El Chapo. If Ty fucked up now, it would cost him his life and Shai's too. Meno had been doing everything in his power to not let anything happen to her. He had rehearsed this conversation for a day now, and it was time to tell her.

"Shai, you must listen carefully to me. You are in danger. After I get off the phone, you must throw it away. Stay off this phone, get another one." Meno paused, he started to act out his sorrow for her. "Everything you know of Ty is dead."

"No," Shai yelled into the phone. She gripped the sheets tightly and anger ran through her like a jolt of electricity.

"Yes," Meno said. "You must not surface like before, you are in danger, you and Moni." Meno stopped to catch Shai's attention. "Are you listening?" he asked. "You and Moni will disappear. When you get another phone, call me, and we will keep in touch." Meno waited for her to speak.

Shai was quiet.

"I'm sorry, my Shai!"

Shai's tears were enough to tell Moni what had happened without speaking. Moni just bowed her head to her legs and began to cry. By the time Rell reached his lawyer and made bond so he could call, Shai had soaked her tears up with the sheets and put her clothes on. She turned the phone off and dumped it in the hospital trash can, then left.

Chapter One

I walked out of El Chapo's Mansion, to the CLS Benz parked in the front of the house. Chavez was sitting in the car on the phone. He didn't notice me walking up, and he hung up quickly when I opened the door.

"Where we going?" I asked.

"To have a drink," Chavez said, driving off down the long dirt road. We reached the city of Mazatlan, Sinaloa, a city on the west coast of Mexico. El Chapo loved the city, because it was a popular port for U.S. cruise ships. Perfect for drug transportation. From where I had been to here, it looked like night and day. It looked alive and had a Miami feel to it. Chavez drove down North Beach and Camarones. He rolled down the windows and took a deep breath.

"Twelve miles of beach. Surf, sail, waterski, parasail, or be amongst the weak basking in the golden sun." Chavez spit out the window. He continued up the strip, until we reached a restaurant called Los Palapas. It was an elegant restaurant by the beachfront.

The waiter approached the table, and Chavez looked up. "Give me the best tequila you have," he looked at me, "and you my friend?"

"Give me the same," I said. I studied the scenery. Mazatlan was a beautiful place. It was a tourist attraction, which was crazy, because no more than twenty miles away lived one of the most dangerous men in the world. And most of the tourists didn't know it. The waiter brought the drinks and laid some menus on the table, then left. I waited until she was out of earshot.

"So, who is El Chapo's nephew?" I asked.

Chavez looked at me. "What do you mean? He is a nephew, that's all you need to know."

"What if I told you I don't want to do it? How can I get to this person?" I was trying my best to probe information out of him, but it wasn't working.

Chavez just looked at me seriously. "Señor, you have no choice at all." He continued to stare, studying my expressions. "Let's go, you may need to loosen up." He got up from the table.

He took me to Valentino Disco. The Disco looked like a huge mansion that sat on an island around rocks. The outside of the building was all white, with colors throughout the inside. Silk lay across everything. Beautiful women were everywhere, dancing and staring as soon as we stepped inside. Chavez was very popular. The ladies flocked to him, rubbing his face and neck. The men shook his hand and greeted him with respect. Several guys that he greeted had the same tattoo on their necks. A tattoo of a scorpion.

I followed Chavez's motions as he greeted the others. When we sat down, I felt out of place like a motherfucker. Each minute I thought to myself, "What the fuck am I doing?" Now I knew where the statement "the game chose me" came from. We drank, and I sat listening to them discuss business. It was a very political argument over territory. I mean, we fought over blocks back home, killing each other for two streets and some colors, or a rundown dope spot that we didn't even own. But these motherfuckers in here talked about states and regions, East coast and Midwest, and shit like that. The men left after the discussion. Then Chavez turned to me.

"Your loyalty is appreciated," he said, "that's why you're here. Even El Chapo recognizes you. See the man who just left, there's no loyalty, only greed. You was just in the presence of three Cartel representatives. Juarez, Sinaloa, and Tijuana." Chavez looked me in the eyes.

I noticed there was some girls headed in our direction. Chavez waved his hand in the air without looking up, and the guard stopped them from coming past the ropes. "This on-going drug war must cease, and El Chapo is not the type to give in. He's the one making it hard for the others, there is no money in war. So what do we do? Let the other Cartels combine and come at us?" Chavez paused. "Or do we get rid of the problem ourselves?"

* * *

Rell pulled up in front of Ty's home after leaving his own. There was no sign of anyone. He tried the door, but it was locked. He crept around the side of the house to the private gates and started to check windows. His phone went off, and Rell tried to stop the beeping before anyone heard him in the backyard. It was Boo saying he had gotten all the money from the safe houses and was at the crib. The old man had been watching him since he pulled up.

"I left the back door unlocked," the old man said.

Rell looked up at the old man.

"I left the back door unlocked, just in case somebody came back," the old man repeated.

Rell walked to the back door and opened it. The old man followed him inside.

"I seen you around the youngster a lot," the old man said, "so I figured I'd let you know that I got all of the valuables over at my house. The cops been here looking around, asking questions. They said there's a federal investigation going on." The old man kept talking.

Rell listened and walked around, looking at the stains on the carpet in the corridor of the living room.

"I haven't seen the girls either," the old man said. "Yeah, they took out three of them on stretchers, I think they didn't make it out."

"Three? Shit," Rell mumbled under his breath.

"Some Mexicans came and took the youngster after—" Rell cut the old man off.

"Some Mexicans?" Rell asked.

"Yeah, they said some El Chapo wanted him, and they took him. Shit, I thought I had the drop on one of the motherfuckers until red dots started popping up all over my ass. I dropped that gun quick as a mafucka. Wherever they took him, it can't be good."

Rell checked the rest of the house.

"Let me get they shit," Rell said to the old man.

"Come on."

They walked over to the old man's home. Rell packed all their belongings into the car.

"If you find the youngster, tell 'im I said stop by sometime," the old man said as Rell was getting into the car.

"I got you," Rell said as he pulled out the driveway.

* * *

Rell grabbed the boxes out of the car and went inside. Chad and Boo got up soon as he opened the door.

"What's up? Who shit is this?" Chad asked, walking over to help.

"Ty's and Shai's shit," Rell said.

"Where they at? What happened?" Boo asked.

"Man, I don't even know. I checked everywhere. Hotels, hospitals, and morgues."

"Morgues? What the fuck you mean?" Chad said, dropping the box.

Rell told them what he saw at the house. He told them about everything that had happened before, and told them about the bloodstains. He could tell they were mad as hell. They paced back and forth while Rell told them what went on.

"I'mma go to Phoenix in a couple days," Rell said. "Y'all gon' come with me. I think that's where Ty at." He knew trying to track

Ty down in Phoenix was a long shot, but he had a few connections that might help him out. "Meanwhile, we gotta get this money out of here. Y'all went to all the spots and got all the change?"

"Yeah. Shit, where you gone hide all this dough, nigga?" Chad asked.

"We gon' have to put it up in a safe house until we able to find out what's up," Rell said. "Get a couple of stacks for the trip, because finding Ty gon' cost us some change."

Chapter Two

Within hours of the phone call, Shai and Moni had cut all ties with the world. They were in Eureka, Missouri. Eureka sat almost one hundred miles outside of St. Louis, down highway 44. The little city held St. Louis Six Flags Amusement Park. They were staying in a nice home under alias names. They had enough money to stay under the radar for years. Even if they needed money, Meno was always there. They were used to staying out of sight. They'd had to do this before, when they were young. It was a fun time for them. Shai called it a rush. But this time it wasn't fun. They wasn't young anymore, and they had found people they could settle down with. And that had been taken away from them, all in one night.

They stocked up on groceries, DVDs, and cosmetics, and bought things for the house. When the furniture was delivered, they stayed out of sight, so that the movers didn't see them. They took every precaution not to show their faces.

After the movers were gone, Shai came into the living room and sat down. She was still stressed and hurting from losing the baby.

"Why you didn't tell Chad and Boo where we at?" Moni asked.

Shai shook her head. "Girl, they told Ty about Meno, so I didn't think they would understand this shit right here." Shai thought about it for a minute. "After a while, I'll probably give them a holla."

"Did you get the newspaper out of Phoenix yet?" Shai asked. She searched in the newspapers every day to see if Ty's or Rell's bodies had been found. She thought about checking down in Phoenix also.

"Yeah, it hasn't gotten here yet, though," Moni said. Moni stayed on the computer. They had decided to keep looking and have hope until the bodies popped up.

The doorbell rang.

Shai looked at Moni. Shai grabbed the tech that was stashed under the pillow by her, and they scrambled to the door. She stood right by the door, so when Moni open it, if anyone tried to barge in, they would catch shots through the door first.

Moni answered the door with a friendly, disguised voice.

"Who is it?" she yelled, peering through the side window. "It's some lady," she whispered to Shai.

Shai waved her hands at her. "See what she wants," Shai said, still holding position. She didn't trust no one. It could be a girl scout, but she didn't give a fuck at this point.

Moni opened the door.

"Hi, how are you?" Moni said, "Can I help you?" The Caucasian lady looked to be a soccer mom, about in her 40s.

"Hi, my name is Jamie, and I live right next door, and I was just coming over to meet you, that's all, ya know, getting to know the neighbor kind of thing." She extended her hand with a smile.

"Oh, thank you very much, that's kind of you," Moni said, trying to play it off. She hoped the woman wouldn't notice the faint scent of weed on her.

"Thanks, if you ever want to have a house warming let me know, I can bring over something to eat. Or if you ever want to just talk. We tend to have a good relationship with all the neighbors on the block," the lady said.

"Oh okay, well, right now its just me and my sister. And we are still rearranging a bit, so we haven't decided when we will have a house warming, but I'll be sure to let you know as soon as I do." Moni said, stepping back, trying to let her know the conversation was over.

"Well, I hope to meet your sister soon. Oh, I didn't get your names."

Moni tried to hide her facial expression with a smile. "Fuck," she thought, "this bitch is annoying."

"I'm sorry, my sister's name is Amy, and I'm Dasia Thompson," Moni said. Moni could tell she wanted to pry some more. She kept trying to look past her, into the house. The old lady didn't know that if Moni tapped on the door twice, Shai would send a slug straight through her head. And they could pack up and move somewhere clse.

"Nice to meet you too, Jamie, bye!" Moni closed the door, and Shai lowered the gun.

"Damn," Shai said. "You picked a good block, we staying next door to a heal the world bitch." Shai threw the gun back under the pillow.

"It's low key, though, this bitch is the only problem," Moni said, sitting back down at the computer.

Chapter Three

I woke up with a headache. My head throbbed from drinking all the tequila. The shit back home was weak compared to the shit out here. Last night, I'd sat on the balcony thinking about Shai and the baby. I didn't want to believe they were gone. I'd thought about Rell and how he must think something was wrong, because I hadn't gotten at him yet.

I'd been here for almost a week, and I was beginning to think I was being held hostage. I decided to find out what was going on, even though my head still hurt. I walked out of the room.

The house was huge, so I didn't know which direction to go. My room was on the west wing of the estate, so I headed the way I knew. I strolled down the spiral stairs, into the front foyer. I went right from there and found some double doors that sat open to an office. A little blood smeared on the floor, like someone had been dragged out of the office and into another room. I followed the blood down a hall to a large sitting room.

I looked up, and El Chapo was wiping his face with a towel. He looked like he was drunk. His eyes were cold, and he looked as deadly as ever. Everyone looked at me, standing in the doorway. I looked at the man tied to the chair. Around him were various types of weapons that could be used to torture people. Bats, knives, the machete. If you wasn't cut for this shit, you definitely wouldn't want to fuck around with them. They could break most of the niggas I knew.

"Señor Ty, I see you want to join the party," El Chapo walked up and put his arm on my shoulder. He wiped the remaining blood onto my shirt, then patted me on the back. "Come see this pathetic weakling." He grabbed the bat and hit the man in the knees.

The man yelled in agony. "Por favor, Por favor!"

El Chapo pushed him in the face. "Shut up!" He flipped the bat in the air, catching it by the end and leaving the handle pointing to me. "Your turn. This is a person who owes money."

I knew this was a test. Everyone looked to see what my reaction would be. I didn't take the bat. I didn't want to hit someone I didn't know, or someone who hadn't done anything to me. Instead, I took the machete and sliced his hand off. I dropped the machete the same way El Chapo had in the building down the hill and stepped out the room onto the patio area. El Chapo was smiling. The others grabbed their wrists, imagining the pain. El Chapo came out shortly with some guards. He waved them away.

"Have a seat," he said, sitting down. He fired up a cigar. "You know, it's funny that you cut his hand off. That may have saved his life, a message sent." He looked up and smiled. "I want to tell you a story of my uncle." He puffed at the cigar. "My uncle was a very serious man, very feared. He had a cousin that was very arrogant and jealous hearted. Especially to his woman. He loved her. Well, the cousin owed my uncle some money, so my uncle took what he loved the most."

"His wife," I said.

"No!" El Chapo held up one finger. "He took him and had a doctor amputate all of his limbs: arms and legs. Well, when he healed, he was nothing but a body with a head. Then my uncle came to his house one day, picked up his little body and sat him in a chair. Then he went and got his cousin's wife and raped her in front of him. You should have seen how he squirmed and jerked his shoulders like he wanted to rip my uncle apart." El Chapo laughed.

I thought about what he said and started to laugh a little myself.

"It was a joke, Señor!" El Chapo said.

"That's a fucked up joke," I said.

"You have family, Señor Ty?" El Chapo asked.

I knew not to tell this motherfucker about my family at all. That was their tool of punishment, killing families.

"Not really. I got a brother. He's strung out on the pipe, so it's just me and my crew," I said.

El Chapo just shook his head. He probably knew I was lying, but I didn't give a fuck. He wasn't about to hunt down my people. I was an only child, and my parents lost me to the streets at eleven years old. They'd disowned me, since I was thirteen, so I'd been on my own. I hadn't talked to them or seen them since I turned seventeen, almost ten years ago. I'd been hustling hard ever since. I came from a little street pusher to sitting at the table with one of the most notorious drug lords in the world.

"You know, a man of your kind has never sat with me before. You are in my drug war now, and you helped a lot, unknowingly." He held up a finger. "You kept the product flowing, even when we cut you off. You were persistent, and I like that." He got up from the table. "Come with me, I'm going to show you a little persistence of my own." El Chapo waved his hand to me and walked off.

We walked out to the back of the house. Outside, two guards got on dirt bikes and rode off into the hills. El Chapo got in the back of a Jeep, while two other guards hopped in the front. I got in the back with El Chapo, and we followed the dirt bikes. We rode through bumpy dirt paths that had been cut straight through the jungle. The branches and leaves still lay along the path. The heavy scent of marijuana hit me, and before I knew it, we were traveling through a forest of marijuana plants. The road became smooth. Workers in the marijuana fields trimmed, cut, chopped, and piled the plants. They wiped sweat from their heads. They looked like they been there for days. Women, men, and some looked like children.

We came to a stop in front of a large building. El Chapo hopped out of the Jeep.

"Ven aqui," he yelled to one of the workers standing nearby. The worker rushed over and opened the doors. They were huge, like airplane hanger doors. He slid them back, and I saw piles of cocaine and marijuana all over the place. Workers packaged it and stacked it along the walls and pallets. Bales of marijuana and kilos of cocaine were compressed and wrapped. I couldn't believe how much work I was looking at. You could get high as fuck just from standing in there.

El Chapo was signing some papers like this was a legitimate business. Like this was Anheuser-Busch, shipping beer out to stores and shit.

"See, this is my persistence," he said, lifting his hands up twirling around. "This is the meaning of persistence, never running out, no matter the consumer; never stopping, no matter the war; and never giving up, no matter the pressure." He walked up closer to me. "You choose to give this up and die, then you've insulted my presence and everything I've shown you. This is the best of the best."

I walked around, looking at some of the product. The coke looked good. I could smell it and tell. I looked at some of the weed and noticed it was some bullshit brown with a lot of seeds. A lot of bales were like that.

"This shit ain't the best right here." I said to El Chapo.

El Chapo walked over to the bales of marijuana. "What is this?" he yelled at the guy packing it. El Chapo snapped his fingers at one of the guards.

The guard reached in his pocket and gave him a knife. El Chapo cut open several bales of weed. All of the bales was packed with the bullshit.

"Where is my mota?" he hissed at the guy that was packing the weed. He smacked him, then backhanded him.

The guy pointed to the barrels in the corner. El Chapo walked up and pushed one over. The lid rolled off, revealing light green buds of marijuana. It was filled to the top with weed. El Chapo rushed and popped the lids on all the barrels and found all of his marijuana. It had to have been thousands of pounds.

The guy knew he was about to die. He didn't try to run. He picked up a machete and swung it at me. I guess he was going for the motherfucker responsible for getting him caught.

I leaped back right in time. He was so close he cut a piece of my shirt. The blade got stuck in a bale of weed, and before he could free it and gear up for another swing, I two pieced him.

He fell back into the barrel of weed. The guards rushed him and held him up. El Chapo walked over and patted me on the shoulder, while looking at his prisoner.

"Very good, Señor Ty. You just saved me millions and found a rat for me to exterminate. So for my gratitude, I give you the pleasure." He picked up the machete.

"Damn," I thought, "they don't use guns around this bitch!" I looked at the machete, then I looked at the guy.

He wasn't showing no fear at all. Matter of fact, he was mugging me. One of the guards had a gun on his belt, so I snatched it. Then I grabbed the guy by the neck, turned him around, and kicked him to the ground. I fired three shots into his head. I gave the guard his gun back.

This shit was making me dangerous. I was beginning to have no respect for life at all. Just being here with El Chapo made me feel untouchable. I could get away with anything here, and I was utilizing that.

"If that shipment would have made it out, I would have lost millions, and it would have set me back," El Chapo said. He waved to the guard, then walked off to talk with him in private.

I watched as the workers stared at me.

"Come, let's go," El Chapo said as he hurried past me out the door.

Chapter Four

Rell, Chad, and Boo landed in Phoenix. Rell had a bitch out here that he used to fly out to the Lou sometimes. He called her up soon as they landed. It'd been a while since they hollered, and he hoped this was the number still. A woman picked up the phone, she sounded a lot older.

"Hello," she said.

"Hey, is Catalina there?" Rell asked.

"Yes, hold on," The woman said.

Rell could hear the old lady yelling Catalina's name, and he could also hear kids crying in the background. He thought she'd probably had a couple of shorties since they last fucked around.

"Hello, who is this?" Catalina asked.

"This Rell! What's up?"

"Oh, hey! How you doing?" she said in a friendlier tone.

"Shit! Just got into town and decided I'll hit you up and see if we could get a bite to eat," he said. He was hoping she would come and sit with him, because he would hate to have to kidnap the bitch.

"That's cool, where you staying?" she asked.

Rell gave her the hotel, and room number. They were staying at a La Quinta Inn. He would have stayed at the Residence or the Hilton, but they were here on business, and they had guns on them.

Chad and Boo both had gun licenses, so they could travel that way. They didn't care about using them though, because they were never going to find them anyway.

"A'ight, call me when you pull up out front," Rell said, then hung up the phone.

"Damn! You should've told her to bring some friends," Chad said.

"Nigga, we trying to find Ty!" Rell said.

"I know! But that don't mean we can't get no pussy!" Chad said jokingly. He was bullshitting with Rell. He knew there was no room for error. No time to fuck off.

Ty and Rell had been homies since the streets took them. So Rell was going to avenge Ty's death if he was dead. Rell didn't believe he was dead, though. He knew Ty too well, and no matter the situation, Ty could get out of it. The phone rang an hour later. It was Catalina. Rell got up.

"Hey, I'm bout to go with this bitch and see what's up," Rell said as he walked out the door.

* * *

Me and Chavez were on our way to the private jet. El Chapo had instructed Chavez to take me to Phoenix and introduce me to all the resources. After that, we were to fly to California and meet some more people.

"You have entered a whole new world, Señor Ty," Chavez said as we sat down on the plane. "You are no longer Ty, to us, you are El Moreno." Chavez laughed. The others started to laugh also.

"El Moreno," one of the guys said nodding his head in approval. I knew a little Spanish, but El Moreno went over my head.

"What's El Moreno?" I asked.

"Well, since you are not Mexican, and you are family, it's just like saying the brown Mafia Mexicana." He chuckled.

I started to laugh also. "Yeah, El Moreno, I'm cool with that."

The flight to Phoenix was quick. We landed and went to the house of a short Mexican named Puncho. He talked fast and moved around like he was high on speed or something. Chavez introduced me to everyone as El Moreno. They laughed at first, then nodded in approval.

"El Moreno, you do very well for the family, eh," Puncho said, smoking a cigarette.

"I do what I can," I said.

Puncho looked at me nodding his head up and down.

"Whenever you're in town, stop by, okay?" he said, shaking my hand as we left. We went by a few other spots in Mesa and South Phoenix. Everyone greeted me with respect and told me to come around whenever I was in Phoenix. The last spot was Meno's.

Meno was out front waiting for me. Soon as I got out the car, he greeted me with a hug and looked at me like I was a son he hadn't seen in years.

"Señor Ty, how are you?" Meno said. "Come in, we must talk."

Chavez was getting back into the car.

Meno waved, then looked back at me. "Don't worry, you will be staying here with me. We will have dinner." We strolled into the house.

I was glad I was around someone that might have had contact with Shai or Moni. And I was glad I was back in the U.S. I could go get some clothes now, too. I was tired of wearing slacks and wifebeaters. I looked like a Mexican gang member.

We sat down on the sofa in his office area. I was impatient to find out what had happened to Shai.

"Have you heard from Shai or Moni?" I asked.

Meno's face grew tight, and he looked saddened by my question.

"You don't know. Shai and Moni," he paused. "My Shai is gone." He bowed his head.

I looked at him in disbelief for a moment, then leaned my head back on the sofa. It didn't surprise me to hear it; it was just that I had almost fooled myself into believing that they were still alive.

"When I find the bodies," he said, "we will have a proper burial." He looked at me.

I couldn't hold back the tears. They trailed down the side of my face as I stared at the ceiling.

"You really loved my Shai?" he asked.

Meno wanted to tell Ty about Shai, but he thought Ty wouldn't be able to leave her alone and keep their relationship a secret. So he kept it a lie.

"Let's have a drink," Meno said. "To my Shai and Moni, and to a new friendship in business." Meno toasted.

I didn't move at all. I was stuck in pain. I eventually downed the shot and sat back down on the sofa. I was angry that I couldn't do nothing. The person I thought that was responsible was dead already. The way I felt, I wanted to exhume his body and chop it up the the machete.

* * *

Rell and Catalina sat at the table in Joe's Crab Shack in Tempe, AZ, a small subdivision in Phoenix. Rell didn't order anything, he let her do the ordering. The big bucket of crab legs just sat there getting cold. He was contemplating how to approach her for help. He seriously didn't want to poke the bitch with the icepick.

"Why you not eating?" Catalina asked. "You ain't hungry?"

"Naw! I'm cool, just chilling," Rell said.

Catalina wasn't buying that. She smirked a cheap grin, like "yeah, right," then continued cracking her crab legs.

"Can you crack this one for me, papi?" she asked, handing him the leg and the cracker. "Why you haven't called me? What you been up to?"

"Shit! The same ole thing," Rell said.

"What's up? What's going on?" she asked dropping the food and the utensils.

Rell looked at her. "I need you to do something for me," he said.

"Whats that?" she replied, frowning her face up.

"I need you to get me in touch with Meno." He leaned in a little closer to her, "I need you to find out where he's stayin'."

She leaned back and looked at him like he was crazy. Then she got up from the table and started to grab her things and headed towards the door. Rell threw a hundred dollar bill on the table then quickly followed her. She walked fast to her car.

"What the fuck wrong with you?" Rell shouted, rushing after her.

"No! What the fuck is wrong with you?"she yelled. "What you trying to do? You're trying to get me killed like Heather. I'm not going out like that bitch!"

Rell didn't even know Heather was dead. He walked over to her to try and calm her down. She backed up until she backed into a parked car.

"No," she whispered as Rell looked into her eyes. She could tell he was desperate.

"Come on, just point me in the right direction," Rell said, putting his arms around her. "You know I ain't gon' say ya name."

Catalina bit her bottom lip. She still couldn't resist Rell. She always hoped to be with him one day, but he'd never acknowledged her as a companion. Every time she flew into St. Louis to visit him, it was for sex only. So him holding her now, it felt good to her.

"I know this guy named Puncho, he is friends with Meno," Catalina said.

"Cool. Where he be at?" Rell asked.

Catalina looked to the sky.

"Where he be—" Rell was about to repeat it.

"He stay in all Mexican neighborhood, you cannot get to him. And this information alone can get me killed," she snapped. Rell looked around to make sure no one was looking or listening.

"I'll get to him, where?" he asked again. He was about to reach for his icepick, he was getting tired of the bitch.

Before he took his hands off of her to reach for it, she told him where Puncho lived. She gave detailed directions, how to get to his house, along with the address. Rell wanted to get on top of it A.S.A.P., but he knew he had to treat her ass tonight. If he just left her, it was a strong possibility that she could alert Puncho to him. So he figured he'd kick it with her tonight.

"Come on, let's go finish eating," he said. Catalina wiped her eyes and followed Rell back inside the restaurant.

Chapter Five

Meno and I had been drinking since he told me the news. We both were drunk. He was telling me the stories about Shai at a young age. Every word he spoke, he slurred.

"I always knew she use to sneak in my bedroom and play with the guns. They would always be misplaced." He paused and had a hiccup. He had a sad face expression. "I wish she wouldn't have though." I already talked to him about everything Shai had told me of him.

I asked. "She ended up saving ya life, right?"

He looked at me. "Señor Ty, I was never going to die." He got up and stumbled to the bar. " I owed moncy, a dead man can't pay. So they sent to kill my wife, in doing so, Shai killed them." He sat at the bar and poured another drink. "And she been hiding ever since. They wanted to kill her for her actions. So I told them she was my wife sister, and I had to kill a woman to show them." He drank the shot. "That's why I never said she is my daughter."

It was all making sense to me now. Shai had a hit on her since she was eleven years old. Meno got back up and stumbled back over to me.

"Señor Ty, if you ever have family, keep them totally from business," he said, then walked out the door.

I got up. I was a little tipsy myself. I could walk straight though. I wanted to go shopping for some clothes to get my mind off of things, but I was shot. I had no money. Everything was back home, wide open for the taking. Then I thought, the phone! I hurried to the phone and called Chad and Boo. Neither picked up.

* * *

Chad sat on the couch, he picked up his phone as it went off and looked at the number. He didn't recognize the number, so he laid the phone back down.

"You gave somebody my number, nigga?" he asked Boo. "What area code is 602?"

"Nigga, that's here." Boo said.

The phone stopped ringing before Chad picked it back up to answer.

* * *

I dialed the numbers twice. I called Moni and Shai, both of their phones were disconnected. Rell's phone was powered off. Chad's and Boo's phones began to go to voicemail as well. I got so mad at the thought of losing all of them, I threw the phone down shattering it to pieces. A guard hurried in the room with his hands on his gun. He looked at the phone then at me. The look on my face made him back out of the door and close it behind him.

* * *

Rell came through the hotel room door. "What up, we got action?"

"You just call me, nigga?" Chad asked.

"Naw! Why?" Rell asked.

"Because, somebody just called from a 602 area code," Chad said, showing Rell the number.

Rell snatched the phone and quickly dialed the number back. It just rang, no one picked up. He tried it again back to back. Still no answer. He decided to lock the number in the phone and call it every hour until someone answered. Rell sat down holding the phone, he had a feeling that was Ty. He sat the phone down and started at it for a while. Hoping it would ring again. Nothing happened!

"Look, get them thangs, we going to see a nigga name Puncho," Rell said, getting up from the sofa.

* * *

Elan sat alone in a hotel room, in Denver, Colorado. He had been running for a week now. All of his people and family were dead. He looked stressed, he had bags under his eyes. He was desperate for some protection. He knew the Mafia wouldn't stop until they found him. He knew too much. He knew who to run to for protection. They would give him complete revenge. His hatred grew every day for the Cartels. He was X'd out. He wanted to go against everyone.

He found the phone book and flicked through the pages until he found what he was looking for. He picked up the phone and dialed the number. A lady picked up.

"Hello, Federal Prosecutors Office, may I help you?" she answered.

Elan sat silently for a moment. "Hello?" the lady said.

"Yes, I want to speak to a prosecutor, I have some information."

* * *

"Which one of them mafuckas is Puncho, nigga?" Boo asked. They were driving by the house that Catalina had told Rell about.

"Nigga, I don't know, she just said he stayed there," Rell replied. "Bend another corner."

Chad hit another block. It was a group of Mexicans hanging out on the corner up the street. As Chad, Rell, and Boo drove up the block, they started to walk out into the street. They tried to look inside to see who was in the car, but couldn't because of the tint on the windows. Rell had tint put on every rental so no one could see him coming through. The Mexicans hurried back to the sidewalk. They whistled to the others, then started to run for their cars.

"What the fuck they on?" Chad asked, he watched them run off as he turned the corner.

"Hit this mafucka, nigga! Lets roll," Boo said.

Chad hit the gas. Before they made it to the corner, a car was in high pursuit. When they were about to turn at the next corner, a car pulled right out in front of them, almost hitting them head on. Chad whipped the wheel, turning into someone's yard. He got around to the other side of the car and smashed off. The Mexicans got out shooting.

"Get down!" Chad yelled, speeding down the street. He swerved out into traffic onto a main road and sped off.

* * *

"Motherfucker!" A woman yelled out of her car window as Chad swerved out in front of her. She was on her way home from work. She stayed in the neighborhood they had just come from. She looked down the street and could see her son chasing after the car that almost hit her.

"What's going on?" she yelled to her son. Her son ran up to the car.

"See where they going," he said in spanish.

She pulled off quickly, trailing behind them.

* * *

Boo, Rell, and Chad got out of the car at the hotel and hurried inside to the room.

"That bitch said it was gon' be hard to get to dude," Rell said, walking to the table. " I don't think she was that stupid to set a nigga up!" He pulled out some weed and rolled up a blunt.

"Nigga, we way down here wit no real straps, trying to run up in a Mexican hood on somebody, tsst," Boo said. He was getting irritated and was ready to go back home. He didn't want to admit this was a bullshit mission they was on. He knew the bond with Rell and Ty was tight. He would do the same for Chad in a heartbeat.

"Don't sweat, we just gotta plan this out," Rell said, taking a hit off the weed. Chad got up and open the door.

"I'm bout to go get some drank and ice, what's up?" Chad asked. "We need to go and switch the whip up anyway."

Rell and Boo got up, and Rell grabbed the weed and the icepick and headed out.

* * *

"Who was it, you know?" Puncho asked the young boy that was there earlier chasing after Rell, Chad, and Boo.

"No, I couldn't see them!" The boy said. "My mom followed them though, they staying at the La Quinta Inn off Bates," he said.

Puncho was getting tired of the blacks ripping him off. Just recently they kicked in one of the stash houses in the neighborhood. They got away with twenty kilos of coke and 400 pounds of weed. That had to come out of his pocket. He started to have lookouts posted on every corner watching for unfamiliar cars.

Puncho gritted his teeth as he spoke to one of his guards. "Send someone over there to take care of these motherfuckers!"

* * *

Chad, Rell, and Boo pulled back into the hotel parking lot. They had switched cars already. Chad pulled around to the back of the hotel.

"Someone's been in the room!" Boo said.

Rell looked up and noticed the door was slightly open.

"Back up and park on the other side," Rell said.

"Peep it out!" Boo said as he noticed a Mexican waiting in a car several rows down.

Rell didn't waste no time. He got out and crept around the back of the car. He had a gun in one hand and the icepick in the other.

He ran around the side of the car and pointed the gun to the Mexican's neck. He cupped the icepick in his other hand. Before the Mexican could move or get a word off, Rell hit him twice with his icepick. Once in the chest, once in the neck. He slid to the back of the car crouched down. He didn't want to start a shoot out in Phoenix, plus there was nowhere for him to run, so he backed away and hopped back in the car with Chad and Boo. They drove off. The guy Rell hit got out the car holding his wounds. He stumbled to the door of their room where his crew was searching and collapsed in the doorway.

* * *

I was tired of drinking and waking up with these headaches. I got up, showered, and put on the same shit I'd had on for three days now. Scottsdale had an outside designer mall I had to get to. It was around the corner from Houston's, where all this shit kicked off. Elan! I thought about Elan, that snake mafucka. I needed to get out and ride around, free my mind from all this bullshit before I cracked. I walked through the house looking for Meno. He was nowhere to be found. Damn.

I saw some guys sitting on the veranda.

"Hey. Where Meno?" I asked.

They looked up.

"El Moreno, Meno is gone. What's up?" one of the guys said.

"Where the keys to the car? I need to go get some more clothes and shit." As I was talking, Chavez walked out on the varanda.

"El Moreno. Fellas." He greeted everyone.

"Just who I need!" I said, pointing to Chavez. "Run me to the mall, so I can get out this shit."

"Okay. We can do that on the way to Puncho's house. I have some business over there," he said. We left the house and got into his truck.

"What type of clothes do you prefer?" he asked, closing the door to the Range Rover.

"Shit! Gucci, Louie, Prada, ya know! That kinda shit!" I said.

We finally reached the stores. I let Chavez know I didn't have any money, and he reached into his pocket and pulled out a Black Card. I bought ten outfits and ten pairs of shoes. I didn't know how much longer I was going to be here. The first thing I picked out, I put right on and left the other shit in the dressing room. I just pulled off the tags and gave them to the cashier to ring up.

I piled the bags into the back of the Rover and we left for Puncho's spot.

"So what's going on?" I asked. I felt a lot better now that I was in some shit that I liked. The clothes, the rides, now I just needed to get back to the Lou and take over like Hova.

"There has been a situation going on," Chavez said. "No offense to you, but it is with the blacks. They have been robbing our safe houses. Puncho thinks some more have been scoping out the neighborhood again."

I could understand where Chavez was coming from. It was no offense to me. It was part of the game. It didn't matter the color, them pistols was colorblind. If they was trying to hurt my family then so be it. They die.

We finally pulled up to Puncho's home. He came out and greeted us. "El Moreno, I didn't expect to see you. How's it

38

going?" Puncho said in his normal speedy tone. "Come on! We have to talk!"

We went inside of Puncho's home. It was not what I expected. He was a real hustler. He had people everywhere, and there was a strong odor of drugs in the house. Several guys sat on the couch in the living room. They watched TV on the plasma that Puncho had sitting on the wall. There were three big ones, side by side. One for regular television, one for the Spanish news station, and one was a security monitor.

We walked past the kitchen towards the back rooms. There were guys in the kitchen packing coke. There was a room full of weed, then a room full of heroine as we continued down the hall. Guns were all over the place. Guns were leaning up against the walls, the dressers, and the tables. We went into a back room that had only an office chair and a table with a sofa next to it. It looked like they counted money in this room. We sat down on the sofa, while Puncho sat down in the chair.

"You know someone hit us two weeks ago," Puncho began. "Well, yesterday more guys came through here. Looked like they was scoping out the spot. We had them followed after we chased them out of the neighborhood, and they were staying at the La Quinta Inn off Bates." Puncho took out some cigarettes and fired one up. "I sent some of my men to deal with these motherfuckers, and one of my guys got fucked up. Someone hit him with an icepick." Before he got to say the next word, I stopped him.

"Hold on! Hold on! An icepick?" I said, as I wondered.

"Yeah! The motherfucker hit him in the neck and chest," he said, showing the area his guy was hit in. "We had to get rid of his ass, so we finished him off and dumped him off in a alley."

I thought to myself, an icepick. That had to be Rell. Sticking mafuckas with a icepick wasn't a new trend. I wanted to say that I might know who did it, but I didn't want to raise no suspicions.

"This is a problem we must deal with, before they think we're too weak for them," Chavez said.

Puncho just nodded his head in agreement.

"Let me deal with it," I said, looking at Chavez. "Maybe I can get up on them better than y'all can."

Chavez looked at Puncho. "El Moreno is demonstrating the family traits." Chavez extended a hand out to me.

I got all the information from Puncho I needed. The make of the car, color, and the room number where the guys stayed. I knew it wouldn't help, though. Rell had already switched cars and hotels by now. The only way I could find out how to get in contact with him was through that bitch Catalina. I knew he hollered at her.

After talking with a couple of guys, I found out how to get in touch with Catalina. She worked for a Mortgage Company off Indian School. Me and Chavez went over to pay her a visit. We pulled up. I turned to Chavez.

"Let me go holla at her," I said.

"Go ahead," he replied.

I got out the car. Chavez thought this was a bitch I fucked with. When I walked inside, she almost spilled the coffee she was pouring.

"Ms. Alvarez," her boss called. He was a tall, fat, bald guy.

She looked back at him, then back at me. "Ty! What are you doing here?" she asked with a distraught look on her face.

"You know why I'm here," I said as I walked closer to her.

"Where's Rell?" I asked. She backed up, she probably thought she was good as dead.

"He made me tell him, I—" she said.

"Where's Rell at?" I asked again in my demanding tone. I spoke low so no one would pick up on our conversation. "Call him!"

She got her phone out and dialed the number. Rell picked up.

"Hello! What's up?" he answered. She gave the phone to me immediately.

"What up, nigga?" I said.

"Ty?" Rell replied. "Man! Where the fuck you at?" Rell asked excitedly. "I'm on my way, nigga!"

"Look homie, you can't come where I'm at. You gotta get back to the crib. That shit you did yesterday, they looking for you, and I can't stop it, so go back to the crib until I send for you. Make sure you answer ya phone when I call. It might be tomorrow or something, but I gotta send for you from out there, so they won't suspect nothing!"

"A'ight! We on the next flight out," Rell said.

"We?" I asked. I was praying he was about to say Moni and Shai.

"Yeah. Chad and Boo on deck."

"Yeah, okay, well tell them niggas what's up and start answering they phones," I said.

"A'ight! One!"

"One!" I hung up. I gave her back her phone. "Don't say shit about Rell, and I won't say you ratted them out," I said to her.

She took her phone and shook her head quickly.

Chapter Six

Damn, my nigga back on deck, I thought as I was getting back in the ride. Chavez was on the phone as usual. He was speaking in Spanish. He switched to English. "Yes! I will notify him right now." It sounded real important. Chavez hung the phone up and mumbled something under his breath.

"What's up?" I asked.

"We've just been informed that a rat has given information to the government about most of the Cartels. We don't know who and how serious it is yet, but it's a problem."

Damn, somebody snitching, I thought to myself. I really didn't want to be caught up in that shit. We headed back to Meno's place. When we went inside, they all were watching the news coverage on the Drug War in Juarez. They were also reading the ticker at the bottom of the screen that read: F.B.I. spokesperson said they may have possible information that may lead to the arrest of several top Cartel leaders. This maybe the crack into the Drug War needed to end this violence.

The atmosphere in the room was tense. Eyes were locked on the television, while everyone wondering amongst themselves who could be the informant. The phone rang and Meno picked it up.

"Si," he answered. He didn't say much after that, he just listened as whoever spoke on the other end. He hung up and walked over to me and Chavez. "I've just been informed that it is

Elan," Meno said. "This can very well cripple all of the Cartels! He must die fast!"

"The Cartels have already arranged a meeting between the representatives. We are to meet tonight in Mexico, so I have to go," Chavez said. He walked out of the door, and I followed behind to grab the bags out of the back.

"Señor Ty, it is best that you stay clear of the situation until this blows over. It is very delicate. If someone was to even drop a sweat, they will die," Chavez said, then got into his truck and pulled off. I walked back inside and went up to one of the rooms. Meno came in shortly after me. I thought everything was over, this was it. The end of my run.

"So what's happening now?" I asked.

"Nothing! This just puts others in position, depending on what is said. I may have to disappear to Mexico, and someone will come over and take my place." Meno said.

"What about Elan?" I asked.

Meno looked with a devilish grin. "Elan will die fast!"

* * *

Shai got up early. She walked down the stairs and into the kitchen to get her some orange juice. The doorbell rang. She didn't scramble, she knew who it was. If it wasn't Jamie, it was Carol. Both of the nosy neighbors were beginning to get on her nerves. She took a peep out, then she finally answered the door.

"Hi," Carol said, cheesing from ear to ear and holding a newspaper in her hand. Carol was a red-headed soccer mom in her late 30s. "The mailman delivered this to me yesterday, my husband just notified me of it today, so I'm sorry! Did you all used to stay in Phoenix or something? I was just wondering why would you want a Phoenix newspaper?" she said.

Shai held back her words and frustration. She wanted to snap and say, "Look, you nosy-ass bitch, get the fuck off my porch before I kill yo ass," but she bit her tongue once again.

"Thank you! We have family there, that's all! I'll make sure I check up on the mailman and get the address corrected so it won't happen again!" Shai said instead.

"Oh! It's no problem," said Carol.

"I bet it ain't," Shai thought. "Give yo' ass one mo' reason to come over." She closed the front door before Carol could utter another word.

Moni was in the hallway of the foyer, listening and shaking her head.

"We gotta get the fuck outta here," Shai said. She was irritated and angry. She had been having reoccurring dreams of Ty and her mom. Plus, it didn't help that it was that time of the month.

"You wanna go out East? You know my cousin out there in Baltimore," Moni said.

"I don't care! Let's just go!" Shai was just ready to get away to somewhere that she could breathe a little.

"Alright! I'll get everything together and find us a spot tomorrow," Moni said, grabbing the laptop.

* * *

Despite the news about Elan turning informant, I was feeling better now that I got in contact with Rell, Chad, and Boo. I was back with a family now. Since I left home, Rell had been the only family I'd ever had. We were like brothers; nothing could ever come between us. Even with the street shit, we would never be a G-money and Nino. I wanted to hit Rell up, but it was best we stayed off the lines for a while, until this shit blew over.

If Elan was snitching, I wanted to see how much political and judicial influence the Cartels had. How would they deal with this situation? I felt it was over with. Me, Meno, and everybody was going down. If I was mentioned, then I would just flee like Meno over to Mexico, fuck it. Rell was kept unknown to this shit, so I could still touch his hands from over there. I felt like the grind was at rock bottom. No money was coming in. I had lost Shai and Moni. The guys was back home doing nothing but waiting on me. I was stuck here! Waiting. I was ready to get it back popping and get the streets on lock again. I felt deep down that Elan was their problem, not mine.

I changed clothes, then got the keys from a guard to one of the S600 Benz's. I told Meno I was going out for a while. He wasn't tripping. He was too busy looking at the coverage on the news. I hopped in the Benz and hit the stroll on Van Buren. A bunch of old schools rode by, hitting they hydraulics with the tops down. They were a bunch of niggas chunking up the deuces at me. I threw my two fingers up while stopping at a red light. One of the old schools pulled up along side of me. It was a root beer '63 Impala, with some chrome 13-inch Daytons and trimming. The driver was a female. She was a decent looking chick at that. Looked like she was a real hood bitch though.

"You riding that right there, homie?" the passenger said, blowing out his weed smoke. He was slumped down real low in the ride. I could hardly see him.

"What's poppin' tonight?" I asked. I wanted to know where all the blacks hung out. "The Elks 99. That's where we headed, pimpin," he said, then the chick smashed off. I stayed back a little, I didn't want them to know I was following them to the club. I just wanted to hear some music and see some bitches. Ugly, fat, skinny I didn't give a fuck. It seemed like I been locked up, and I just got out.

The Elks 99 was packed! It was old schools lined up, new rides sitting on dubs, tricked out rides with the plasmas everywhere! They was doing it big down here. I pulled into the parking lot, creeping in line with the other rides, watching the chicks walk past, going into and out of the club. The S600 stood out from the rest of the cars. I was feeling myself! I leaned back into the seat and turned my music up.

The chicks down here wore catsuits a lot. One broad had on a catsuit with her back out, showing the top of her ass cheeks. I didn't think they was gon' let her in the club with that outfit on. Some of the broads was fucked up though. I could tell this wasn't a upscale spot. It was one for the hood. Just based on the crowd outside, I decided I wasn't going in. No pistol, by myself, in a hood spot full of niggas I don't know, and I was in a Benz. Shhiiitt! Never. I was tripping riding through. I circled back around the parking lot. A group of chicks was walking out the club. They didn't look as fucked up like some of the other bitches I had seen. But they wasn't all that either. One of the chicks body was banging though. She had on a short dress. It came up above her knees and just below her ass. She was a chocolate bitch too, thick to death. The one that was looking the hardest at the Benz, was thick, but she looked like she smoked blunts all day. And she looked like if I said the wrong thing, she would be ready to bang on sight. She bent down to see who was inside with me.

"Damn, can I ride with you, baby?" she asked.

I just smiled and kept creeping.

"Damn! You aint gon' stop, nigga?" she yelled.

I looked back out my rear window and thought to myself, "Hell, naw!" I kept creeping. The traffic came to a stop. The chicks once again was walking alongside the ride. I could hear the chick talking,

"Nigga, think he all that cuz he in a Benz, it probably ain't even his," she said, loud enough that I could hear her.

I just laughed a little.

She bent over and showed me her ass. "You could've," she said as she lowered her skirt. As if I was in for a hell of a treat.

"I wouldn't," I yelled back.

She looked back at me and threw her middle finger up. I was so busy tripping off this bitch, I didn't notice the car keeping its distance from me. I pulled off from the club lot. I came to an intersection on 47th Ave as I looked down at the monitor to search for another satellite radio station.

I rose quickly as I heard tires screeching. I looked out the rearview, thinking someone was about to rear end me, but instead I hear a gun jack, "click-clack."

"Rise up out of that, patna," a nigga said, sticking a riot gauge through the window. "Hurry up, homie," he screamed. Another car sped around us, blowing its horn.

"Yeah, nigga," the bitch from the club parking lot yelled as her and her friends drove past.

I threw my hands up, and the gunman opened my door.

"Come on let's roll, nigga," he said.

I was for sure I was about to get popped tonight. I got out the car. He pushed me to the sidewalk and smashed off. I thought for sure they was gon' pop me. Back in the Lou, you didn't get in that sweet. A nigga was gon' pop you soon as he ran up, and on the East Side, you was gon' die getting jacked. Shit fucked me up. Fuck dat car. I looked around, I seen a couple of cars coming up the street towards me. They passed me right up.

I stood on the corner, contemplating which way I'mma go. My phone was in the ride. As I was looking to see if I could find a payphone, a car pulled up. It was one of the bitches I seen in the parking lot. The chocolate bitch that was with the one talking shit. She was driving a Infiniti M45, a new model.

"They took yo' car?" she asked. "You just got jacked?"

"What it look like," I said sarcastically. "Can you drop me off?"

If she wasn't, I was gonna take her shit and leave her ass on the corner, so a mafucka can roll up on her and ask her the same stupid-ass question she just asked me.

"Come on," she said without hesitating.

That made me kind of hesitant to get in her shit. But I needed a lift. She dropped me off at Meno's.

"Damn! This is where you stay?" she asked. She looked out the windshield at the size of Meno's house. "You shitting on me!"

"Naw! This ain't my spot. This a friend of mine's," I replied.

"Oh. Some chick you fuck with, huh?" she said.

A guard stepped out of the house.

"Is that a Mexican?" she asked. "Ooo, you want me to pull off?"

"Naw! Why you don't like Mexicans? He cool," I said, reaching out a hand for her to shake it. "Good looking out," I said. I reached in my pocket to pull out some money. "You need some gas money or something?" I asked.

"Naw! Im good. You can let me get your number, or take mine," she said.

I didn't want to give her the number to the house, so I took her number down.

"I'll hit you up," I said, getting out of the ride. I looked back into the car, and she looked up at me. It was the first time I had actually paid attention to her. She was straight! Dark-skinned with wavy black hair. "What's your name?"

"Oh, Melanie," she said. "What's yours?"

"T," I said. "I'll give you a call a little later."

She nodded, then drove away.

As I walked up, the guard asked me about the car.

"I got jacked," I said. He followed me inside, asking all types of questions. Where? How did they look? What type of car? He was on the phone with the Mercedes Benz alert monitor to try and locate the ride. Shortly after that, Chavez pulled up outside, and all the guards gathered at the front door. The artillery they had looked like some shit from Iraq. Wherever the ride was at, the spot was about to get chopped down.

Chapter Seven

"Check one, clear," a federal Marshal said into his earpiece. Shortly after, another Marshal came over the radio. "Check two, clear." Then four other Marshals walked out with Elan. They had him surrounded on all sides. The prosecutor had offered him complete immunity and a lifetime in the witness protection program. Elan was a valuable piece in the prosecution of the Cartel leaders. If she could, she would've had him stay under her watch at all times.

Elan wanted to be on his own, he was beginning to regret doing this. He'd tried to run twice, but the feds convinced him there was nowhere to run now. Before they got any information from him, they'd leaked his name to the press, that way they was sure he would have no one to go to but them. They were to transport Elan to a small town in the Colorado Mountains. He would remain there until the indictments came down from the Mexican Government and the U.S.

* * *

Chavez waited outside for the guards. He had gotten the information he needed. They mounted up in two vans and drove off. They started to screw silencers on the MP5s, then pulled the ski masks down over their faces. The van came to a sudden halt.

They slid the van door back, running out like it was a police raid. They ran up and kicked in the front door. Chavez walked in after them. He could hear footsteps upstairs.

"You two, check upstair,!" he yelled in Spanish, pointing at the two guards. He looked as one of the guards came out with a little boy. The little boy was Caucasian, dressed in his pajamas. He looked scared as one of the guards held him by the neck with the gun to his head.

"Steven," a woman shouted as she saw her son being held by a stranger with a gun. A guard hit her in the back of her head with his pistol. She stumbled and fell down the steps.

"Mommy," the little boy yelled.

"Shut up," the guard yelled back, gripping the young boys neck tighter while shaking him a little.

"Oww," the little boy mumbled.

Chavez bent down to the woman. He grabbed her by the hair and lifted her head up to him. Her face was soaked with tears.

"Tell your husband, if he ever wants to see his son alive again, then he will take care of our problem for us," Chavez said as he pushed her head back. He got up and waved to the men.

"Nooo," she screamed, as they picked her son up by the neck.

"Mommy," he yelled. The boy kicked and screamed as they forced him into the van. The woman tried to get up, as if to chase after them, but one of the guards kicked her back down while hitting her with the hand gun once again.

"No," she yelled again as she watched her son being taken and forced into the van. "Somebody! Somebody! Please!" She cried as they drove off.

Rell was cruising in his 760 BMW. He had been meaning to get a new whip. He'd had the Beamer for about a year now. He rode around smoking, this was a early morning thing he liked to do. He thought a lot about Moni. He was real bitter over the situation, plus he had been hearing all types of rumors in the streets. That Ty was dead, and they haven't found the body yet. That Rell broke, and the police popped him off. And the worst one that got him heated was that Rell had snitched, got arrested, and now he was out. Rell wanted to catch up with the nigga or bitch who put the rumors out there. And he wanted anybody to ask or say it to him, so he could snap. The more he was seen, the more niggas still asked him for work. Then, when he couldn't produce, niggas started believing the rumors. Chad and Boo had gotten into it with some niggas from the Mac. They was still salty over the T-Mac and Easy situation. Rell knew that wasn't gon' die easy either.

Rell had been bending blocks on the East side lately. He would get up and hit the streets early in the morning. Ride around smoking, then he would go to Helen's and grab a bite to eat. He had to have her breakfast sandwich every morning, it seemed. When he pulled up he saw Fats, a local nigga he was cool with. Fats stayed on the rocks, a area in East Saint off 59th and State Street. Rell looked down at his phone before he got out of the car, he checked it every hour every since he'd left Phoenix to see if Ty had called. He was ready to get it back in.

"What up, boy?" Fats said as he walked upon the car.

Rell got out the ride. "Shit! What's up wit it?" Rell said as they shook and hugged.

"What's been going on? Where my man at? Everything cool?" Fats asked.

Rell knew he was inquiring about the rumors. "Yeah! Everything's straight! Just been fucked up lately." They walked inside and took a seat at the counter. Helen's sat on the rocks, so Fats was a regular there. Helen's was known for her soul food, it had been an after club spot on weekends for the crowd at the Club Casino back in the day.

"Let me get the egg and croquette sandwich," Rell said. Fats ordered his regular, and the lady walked off and started to prepare the meals.

"It's been fucked up around this bitch," Fats said. "Some niggas got it in, but they killing 'em on the weed and white. A nigga can't do shit!"

"Don't trip! A nigga be straight in a minute," Rell said. They paid for the food and walked out.

"Hit me up soon as," Fats said, getting back over to his spot. He turned around and broke off into a sprint when he saw an addict going through his stash, then running off. "Mafucka," he yelled as he caught up with the junkie. Rell watched as Fats beat his ass. Fats picked up the stash he'd tried to run off with and looked back over at Rell. "Hit me up," he yelled.

"I got you," Rell yelled back at him. Rell hopped in his ride and sped off down State Street towards Edgemont. He turned up 84th and crept through the hood. He stopped at the corner of 86th and Martel to finish his sandwich. After he finished, he started to roll up a blunt, then suddenly someone tapped on the window. It was Dame, Los's cousin. Dame was about eighteen or nineteen years old. His cousin used to hustle for Rell, until Rell decided he wasn't built for the game.

Before Rell rolled the window down, he slid his gun to the side of his thigh. "What up, Dame?" Rell said.

"What up, nigga!" Dame leaned into the window. He was looking real scruffy. He looked like he'd had the same clothes on for days.

"Man! Fuck wit me! Let me hold something?" he said.

"What you talking bout, nigga?" Rell replied. He didn't trust Dame at all, especially knowing that he'd knocked his cousin.

"Let a nigga blow one wit you?" Dame said.

Rell looked at the rest of the weed in his personal sack. He knew if he let Dame ride with him, Dame would want to use his phone, most likely to call and let somebody know he had a lick, then he would want to get dropped off at a spot where the goons would be lurking, and then that's yo' ass.

"Here. It's about a quarter zone," Rell said, dangling the bag out the window.

Dame grabbed it and smelled it.

"Damn! What's this shit?" he asked.

"That's purp," Rell said throwing the car in drive. "I'mma holla at you," he said as he pulled off firing up his blunt.

Dame watched Rell as he drove off. He felt he'd played that just right. He knew Rell was responsible for Los being killed. He didn't want to show his hand right then. It would've have been perfect time if he was strapped. He had to get a burna, because the next time he caught him slipping like that, he was gonna knock hit top back.

Chapter Eight

I was getting bored and wanted to get out again. I called up Melanie to see what she was on. The phone rang, then went to the voicemail. I hung up, before I could sit the phone down it rang back.

"Hello," I answered.

"Who is this?" Melanie asked.

"This T," I said. "What's up with you?"

"Oh hey! I thought you wasn't gon' call me for real," she said.

I looked at the phone. "Why you say that?" I asked.

"Because you seemed stuck up! Cocky," she said.

I wanted to get real cocky and ask her for some head and pussy right now. I wanted to fuck and wouldn't mind hitting her thick ass right about now.

"What you doing right now? Let's get up and have a drink," I said. It'd been like a ghost town at Meno's. Ever since Elan turned informant, it'd been no phone calls to each other, no work moving. Everything went underground. I couldn't just stand around here and do nothing.

"I don't care. That's cool," she said. "I'll get ready! You need me to pick you up?" she asked.

"Naw! I'll let you know," I said.

"Okay," she replied.

We hung the phone up. I threw on a fresh outfit and went down to see if there were some keys to a car. I walked in the kitchen, where Rebecca the housekeeper was cleaning. She was an older woman, very nice. I'd talk to her in Spanish sometimes.

"Señor Ty, hello," she said in her best English. I could tell she didn't have her green card. Probably brought over by Meno to work for him.

"Where Meno?" I asked in Spanish.

"He is gone for a while," she said.

"I need a car," I said.

She smiled at me and walked up close to me like she was letting me in on a little secret. She made me huddle down, so she could whisper it to me. I didn't know why. There was no one at home but us.

"Garage out back, the keys are in the hall," she said, pointing to a rack of keys on the wall.

I walked over to the rack and looked at the sets. It was two sets of Benz keys, one set of Rover keys, and numerous other sets that probably went to old schools. Then I saw one set that Meno would be pissed if I got jacked in this one. A Ferrari. I walked out back to see what model it was. I opened the garage, it was a large one. It held at least six to eight cars. Each ride had a tarp over it. I pulled back one that looked like the Ferrari might be under it. I didn't notice what type of car it was, until the back was fully uncovered.

"What the fuck!?" I mumbled to myself. "Damn!" It was a Mercedes Benz SLR, with the gull-wing doors. I'd seen the Benz keys on the wall, but I thought they were to the numerous S-Classes that was driven around here. Fuck the Ferrari! I'm was whipping this tonight! I went in and switched the keys. Rebecca came out behind me to see which one I'd picked. When she saw the SLR uncovered, she said, "Meno like very much!"

"Me too!" I said.

"Okay, Señor Ty," she said, walking back into the house. I opened the door on the ride, it lifted up like it was electronic, folding into the air. I got in and the door came down and closed by itself. I pushed the start button and the engine purred. I ran inside and grabbed the glock that I got last night from one of the guards. I dared a nigga to try me tonight.

I pulled the SLR out to the front of the house. I got to thinking, "Fuck dat bitch, I can go fuck one of the Phoenix Sun's wife with this mafucka. I can come up on the baddest slut in town tonight." Right before I was about to get off into traffic, Melanie hit me up.

"What up?" I answered.

"You want me to come get you?" she asked.

"Naw! I'll come and get you. Where you stay at?" I asked. This hood rat bitch probably stayed in a gang infested area. I really didn't want to drive this in no hood.

"I stay out by the Rain Forrest Mall. It's close to the Airport," she said.

"I know where that's at," I said. "The exit before Bates."

"Yeah! Turn right there at Emerald Drive, and you'll see my car in the driveway."

"A'ight. I'll be there in a minute." I hung the phone up. I meant every word of being there in a minute, because I was about to open this bitch up on the highway and see what she was working with. It had every bit of two hundred on the dash, but I knew they probably had it governed down to about 180 or something. I was about to find out. I took off like a plane. It was a smooth and fast ride. I got on the highway and opened the ride up. I floated past cars like they were parked. I got off on her exit so quick, it took me only five minutes to get from the East of Phoenix to the South. I found Emerald and followed it down until I spotted the Infiniti in the driveway. I was shocked. Her home was nice. She wasn't the normal hood rat, if she was even an official one. I pulled into the driveway and called her phone.

She picked up. "You're here already?" she answered. I saw her look out the bedroom window.

"Yeah! I'm outside," I said.

"That's you in that car?" she asked.

"Yeah! Who else it gon' be?" I replied.

She got silent for a minute. "Well," she finally said, "I ain't ready yet, so you can come in if you want." She opened the front door.

I got out and walked up to the door.

"You forgot to close the car door," she said.

I hit the button on the key fob and the door closed.

"No I didn't," I said as I walked into the house. I stepped inside and looked around.

"You can have a seat," she said.

Her home was well decorated. It was an average home. Nice living room set, kitchen was nice, pictures on the wall. I took a seat. I looked around at the pictures for signs of kids. I didn't see any.

"I'll be back," she said. She walked out of the room. She had on some sweat shorts and a tank top. Her hair was wrapped up like she was just getting out of the shower.

"You want something to drink?" she yelled from the back room.

"Naw, I'm cool," I yelled back. I was tired of that question for real. It seemed like every time that question was asked and I said yes, it was followed by a headache. She came from the back finally.

"There's some orange juice, bottled water, or soda in the fridge," she said.

I was looking at some of the pictures when she walked in. I turned towards her, and damn, she had on a wifebeater and a thong. Her body was flawless. No marks, no scars, and a milk chocolate complexion. Damn! She was pulling her hair back, so the shirt showed her bellybutton. There were no stretch marks, and she had a belly piercing with a diamond in it. I had to think, was this the same chick that I seen that night? The rest of the hood rats made her look bad. Her hair was wavy and silky black, and her eyes were almost hazel. She looked good. Her breasts looked real and firm, a nice palm size. Her firm ass was swallowing the thong. It looked like this bitch did a thousand squats a day. She saw me looking at the pictures.

"That's my brother and his friends," she said. She bent over in front of me. I could see a bit of her pussy through the thong. My dick got hard as hell. "I know you probably thought that was one of my boyfriends or something."

"Naw! I was just looking, like I'm just looking now!" I stared at her pussy. Looking at it from the sides, I could tell she'd shaved.

"Boy," she said as she walked back out of the room. Damn, she was thick as a mafucka ,and she had me ready. I didn't realize how bad I wanted some pussy until now. I wanted to go back there and fuck the shit out of her. But I didn't want to seem thirsty. She came out fully dressed and ready to go minutes later.

"Where we going?" she asked.

"Where you wanna go?" I asked her.

"I don't care, it's whatever," she said. She was dressed nice. A nice casual dress with the back out and laced up. It came up above her knees, but it didn't look too slutty. It showed all of her curves.

"Y'all ain't got a Benihana out here?" I asked.

"No! Where you from? You ain't from here?" she asked.

"Naw! I'm from St. Louis," I said getting up from the couch.

"Y'all got a Benihana out there?" she asked, like she knew already. "Lets go to the Rain Forest Café."

When we walked out, you could see the cars driving by slowing and peeping at the SLR in her driveway. We got in the car.

"Please don't drive too fast. I get scared," She said, trying to fasten her seat belt.

"A'ight," I said, pulling out of the driveway. I crept up the street until I got to the intersection. When the light hit green, I punched it. The tires screeched and the traction snapped into grip and the ride took off.

"Oooh," she screamed at a high pitch.

I slowed down a little. "Damn! You that scared?" I asked.

"Yeah! Don't do that," she said, hitting my arm playfully.

I looked, and her dress had come up to where I could see her thong again. We finally arrived at the Rain Forest Café. We sat in a booth and talked for hours over a meal. The Rain Forest Café was designed to look like a Rain Forest with lots of plants, vines, and background sounds.

"So when you going back to St. Louis?" she asked.

"I don't know for real," I said.

She didn't inquire about why I was here or what I do. I assumed she already knew. That was respectful of her to not try and pry into my business like most broads would. She said she worked as a Company Insurance Assistant. She had a good education and positive attitude. She apologized for the way her friend had acted that night. She had grown up with them, and she'd gone on to college while they'd stayed in the hood on bullshit. She said the other night was her first time in months going out with them. And that it would probably be her last. One of the girls had stolen one hundred dollars from her purse when she went to the bathroom. She said she loved them, but hated their mentality.

I didn't tell her too much about me. She didn't ask much either. When we got the check, she snatched it and paid for the meal and threw the tip on the table.

"I got it! Don't worry," she said. "You can pay for the hotel." Then she walked off.

I hurried behind her. We pulled up to the Hilton, and I got a suite. Soon as we got into the room, she pulled me by my shirt. I reached down and palmed her ass so tight, squeezing it like I was trying to bust it. I pulled the thong out of her ass to the side and slid my fingers inside of her. She started kissing on me more. She went to my neck first, then pulled my shirt over my head and began to kiss on my chest. I tossed the shirt off, and she was already starting on my pants, pulling at the belt like she was trying to rip them off. When she finally got my pants open she pulled them down a little. She gripped my balls and massaged them, while licking her tongue on my dick.

"Damn! I can fuck with this," she said, looking at my dick as it got harder. She started to suck my dick, it was okay. She wasn't no pro. So I let her do her thing for a while, then I pulled her up. I picked her up and threw her legs around me. I slid the dick inside of her. I palmed both ass cheeks in my hands and raised her ass up and down on it. She started to breath heavily, digging her nails into my back. It started to hurt, so I laid her ass on the bed then bent her over.

"Go slow, please," she begged, looking back at me.

I slid it inside slowly and tried to rip her apart. Her ass jiggled and bounced so beautifully, and her pussy was so juicy and wet. It felt so good I couldn't help it. She gripped the cover in her hands and had the pillow in her mouth. She tried not to scream, but let out little ones every other stroke. She shook her head back and forth and hunched her back up to ease up on the pumps. I just held her at the waist pumping her faster, until I busted all over her ass. She laid there rubbing her ass with her eyes closed.

I went into the bathroom to wash up. She came in, wet a towel, put some soap on it, and wiped me off. She cleaned me like I was a Prince or something. She was catering to me hard. The whip probably had her thinking she'd hit the jackpot.

"I feel like lil boosie, wipe me down," I said jokingly.

"Shut up," she said. "You tried to kill me. My stomach still hurting. I told you to take it slow. I ain't out here fucking like that."

"I ain't either," I said.

"Sure. Whatever," she said, walking out of the bathroom. She wiped herself off, then slid back into her dress and put the thong into her purse. "You ready?" she said, fixing her hair in the mirror.

"Yeah." I dropped her back off at home.

As she got out the car, she bent down to look at me. "You ain't gon' walk me to the door?" she said with a frown.

I knew she didn't want me to think she was a freak, because she gave me the pussy on the first date. That shit too late. I went ahead and got out, though.

"So you got what you wanted. I probably won't hear from you, huh?" she said. "Don't get it twisted though, I needed that. That's the only reason you got it tonight."

"Okay, well, appreciate it," I said.

"You better," she said as she walked towards the front door. "Call me whenever!" She said as she closed the door slowly. I know she thought I wasn't going to hit her up, but her pussy was good enough for me to trick on a little.

Chapter Nine

Shai had to get the feel of Baltimore. She had never been there before. She had already gotten used to eating out. She couldn't get enough of her favorite spot, a Brazilian Steakhouse called Fogo De Chao. Every day, she felt more comfortable moving around in Baltimore.

Today, she and Moni were on their way to Obrycki's, a seafood spot. They ordered the crab. The waiter came and dumped a whole bucket of crabs onto the table and gave them a mallet. They laughed as they tried to crack the crabs open. Shai thought of Ty quite often, and Moni thought of Rell, but they knew it was no time to dwell. Their lifestyle didn't promise anything or anyone. They both were good at shielding their emotions.

After eating, they did a little shopping, then headed back out to the county, to their new home. Baltimore was similar to St. Louis, everything went down in the city. The rich lived in Baltimore County, which was nothing like the hood. Shai and Moni had got a nice condo off Reistors Town Road. It was easy to get around, because Reistors ran all the way up to downtown Baltimore through the county.

They had even went out to a club one time already, Windsors. They enjoyed the spot, because it was upscale and laid back. Moni's cousin, Kristy, had been telling them about Club Dream,a five-story club, about forty-five minutes outside of Baltimore, near

D.C. They didn't want to go there just yet. They wanted to get a feel for everything before they hopped out in the streets; plus, everywhere they went, they got hounded by men that saw them in traffic. Seeing two fine chicks in a Range Rover whipping by, while they were riding some bullshit.

Their furniture had arrived, and they finally got everything unpacked. Moni's cousin Kristy stopped by periodically to visit. She was a tall yellow bone. Looked like she could be America's Next Top Model for Tyra Banks. Shai would always tease her, calling her bulimic and anorexic. Kristy was cool, Shai liked her because she kept it real. They all sat watching Paid In Full on their new 60-inch flat screen Moni had put in the family room.

"That nigga bogus," Kristy said, watching the scene where Alpo shoots Rich. "Ooh, every time I see this, it makes me wanna fuck Camron up! I don't even listen to his ass no more."

"Bitch. We was bumping ol' boy the other day," Moni said

"You turn that shit on. Not me! But that is my shit though," Kristy said. "So when y'all gon' hit up Dreams with me? Tomorrow it's going down! Better throw on yo' freak 'em dress and step out y'all," Kristy said, tapping Shai on her arm with a smile. "Girl, it looks like you need some."

Shai was spaced out thinking about Ty. Moni knew where Shai was at. She spaced out too, sometimes.

"You okay?" Kristy asked Shai.

"Yeah! I'm good! But I don't know about Dream, though! It's too many people in there."

"We ain't gotta wait, I got the hook-up," Kristy said.

Shai looked at Moni. She really didn't want to go out to a popular club. She wanted to stick with the low-key joints. But the expression Moni gave her said she wanted to go, and between Moni and Kristy, she was outnumbered.

The next night, they passed by the front of the club. "Damn, it's packed," Moni said. "You sure you can get us in? Cause I'm not about to be waiting in no long-ass line trying to get up in here."

Shai just sat back and looked at the crowd. She was seeing what type of atmosphere it was. The majority of the women were skank bitches looking for hustlers. They had on mini dresses way too short. If they stepped up stairs, those dresses would reveal ass cheeks and pussy. She prayed they wouldn't be on the same floor as her.

Kristy parked and took a look in the mirror one more time before she got out the car. Shai tucked a .25 automatic inside her purse. It was a titanium model, very light weight. They got out and walked through the parking lot. They were all looking their best. Shai wore some Petit Peton sling backs, along with a De'reon outfit. Moni wore a tight fitting Gucci dress with some Gucci jeans underneath. Kristy wore a Pucci Outfit with some Ermillio Pucci strap heels. They got looks from females and niggas that stood around. Groups of dudes was on the lot smoking, drinking, and talking shit. Parking lot pimping. As they passed by, they could hear the comments and hollers.

"Damn, Ma," one yelled.

"What up? Come here, gurl," another yelled.

"Shawty thick as hell, that joint fat, man," some dude said. He had to be from the D.C. area, talking like that. Shai thought them dudes talked real funny. She looked back and laughed when he said that. She looked around at the men on the lot, shaking her head. She thought none of them could hold a candle to Ty. They got to the front entrance, and Kristy waved for the bouncer she knew. A big black gorilla looking dude stepped out the door.

"Hey girl! Who you got?" he asked, letting Kristy by.

"Them two," Kristy said, pointing at Shai and Moni.

"Come on, you owe me," he said, smiling a nasty flirtatious grin. Kristy smiled back a cheap grin and waved at him.

"Damn! Let me find out," Shai said jokingly

"Find out what? Girl, you tripping. I can trick him every time," Kristy laughed.

They got on the elevator and went up to the R&B level. The club was jumping. Keri Hilson's "You Turning Me Off" bumped through the speakers. Everyone was either two-stepping or just vibing. Moni saw a table, so she pulled on the other two to go and have a seat. They ordered some bottles of champagne and a bottle of Hennessy Black. Most of the guys in the club watched them. A few females gave them smirks, probably jealous. Shai and Moni came to enjoy themselves, so they ignored the expressions. As they sat there talking, vibing to the music, some niggas in the club sent over a couple more bottles, but Shai just sent them right back along with two more. She wanted them to know that shit didn't impress them at all.

Kristy put them up on some of the people that was in the club. Some of the freaks that came in to scheme on niggas, and some of the niggas that wasn't on shit. She knew almost everybody. The liquor was getting to them, and they were having fun just sitting talking shit and listening to the music.

Shai threw her glass in the air like she was toasting when she heard the Neyo remix with Fabulous and Jamie Fox. She tried to croon with them, singing the song. "It's cool, I got it, I got it, I got it, I love it when she say—" Shai sang. She got up and moved to the dance floor.

Moni and Kristy joined her. They danced together the whole song, until a couple of guys stepped in and started to dance on Moni and Kristy. They moved to the side of them.

"Excuse me," Moni said.

"What up, yo? I'm just trying to dance with y'all. Y'all over here vibing by y'self. I wanna vibe with y'all," he said. He was short, light-skinned, cocky looking, and dressed in some blue jeans and a V-neck sweater.

"Naw! We good," Shai said.

The dude looked at Shai like he wanted to say something. He just walked away. They started grooving to the music again, and Shai kept an eye on the short, cocky dude. He stood over with his crew, pointing in their direction. She noticed a taller, skinny, light-skinned guy with braids approaching. She acted like she didn't notice him walking up. He walked up and grabbed Shai by the arm.

"Hey! What up, Ma? What's ya name?" he asked.

Shai didn't say anything, she just snatched her arm away.

"Damn! You ain't gotta be like that," he said, smiling. "What y'all diking?" He started to laugh.

Shai ignored him once again. Moni was about to say something, so Shai shook her head towards her, as if to tell her no. Moni was afraid of where Shai was about to go with this nigga. The dude started feeling embarrassed and irritated that Shai was ignoring him. He reached over and grabbed her again, this time he pulled her over to him a little.

Shai stumbled to the side. She had her hand in her purse, gripping the .25, pointing it right at him through the bag. Moni backed up and pulled Kristy with her. She was about to pull the trigger and give him a leg shot, but one of his boys stepped in between them and got in his face. The skinny dude threw his hands up and backed off. The guy that intervened stood there grilling the dude until he went to sit down. He turned to Shai. She was still standing with her hand in her purse with a killer mug.

"Damn! I didn't think anyone as pretty as you could make a face like that," he said. "You look like you was gon' kill him!" This guy was six feet tall, brown-skinned, with an average build. He had on some nice jewelry, a diamond watch, some big-ass earrings, and a diamond chain. He wore some Timberland Boots, jeans, and a nice button down shirt.

Shai just stared at him.

"Hey. My name is Kaleed, but they call me Skills," he said, holding his hand out.

Shai shook it. She still didn't speak. She turned around to walk away.

"Wow! Damn, I look out for you, and I can't get a name?"

"You ain't looked out for me, you looked out for him! Go get his name," Shai said, then she walked off.

After the club was over, they made their way to the truck. As they were walking to the ride, Kristy saw a bunch of dudes over by a van. They looked like they were up to something. They stood around the slide door with their hands under their shirts, like they were holding guns. When one of the dudes came out the slide door with his shirt off, sweating, Shai saw a glimpse of a girl laying on her back with her legs up in the air, and a dude in there fucking her hard. She saw another dude hop in.

"Uh-uh, girl," Kristy said, "they over there fucking the shit out of somebody, straight running a train on her ass. Got her ass all up in the air, going back to back."

"Gon' get you some?" Moni said

"Bitch! You crazy. Never," Kristy said, pushing Moni playfully.

Shai eyed the skinny dude from the club. He stood by the short guy, leaning against a ride. She didn't notice Skills, walking up to her from the other side.

"So, I can't get ya name?" Skills said.

Shai turned around quickly. She had the gun ready this time. The skinny dude tried to reach for his gun, but Shai pointed hers at him, freezing him in motion.

"Damn," Skills said, "I probably did look out for him, huh?" He walked up a little closer, "You wouldn't need to be like that if you had a real nigga in yo corner."

Shai smirked at him. "Oh, and you the real nigga, huh?"

"Damn, give a nigga a chance."

"Shai, lets roll," said Moni.

"Shai," Skills repeated. "Let me call you, Shai, or you can call me whenever." He dropped his card in her purse slowly and backed away.

Shai reached in the purse and looked at the card, then dropped it back into her purse. She walked off, looking at him. She got into the truck.

He passed by on the way out, blowing his horn at them. He was driving a G500 Benz Truck. He nodded at her, seeing the Rover. He threw up a phone to his ear, and mouthed "Hit me up," as he pulled off.

"There you go," Kristy said. "That nigga runs Baltimore."

"I don't give a fuck if he runs America," Shai said, "ain't nothing happening!"

Moni just looked on. She knew Shai wasn't over Ty yet. It would take a while, the same as for her and Rell.

"Well, I'm tired of y'all walking around like niggas, y'all need to get out! Get that stick in you, so y'all can start switching again and start stepping like a diva," Kristy joked.

Moni looked at Shai, and both of them said it at the same time.

"Bitch, fuck you!"

They all started laughing.

Chapter Ten

United States Marshal Ted Harris sat in horror, looking at his wife. He couldn't believe some armed gunman came into his home and took his son. His wife pleaded with him to get their son home safely. He didn't know what to do. All he knew was, if he wanted to see his son alive again, then Elan would have to die. They didn't want no exchange. No Elan for the boy; they wanted him to kill Elan. There was no question that his career, his job, his freedom, and his own life was worth the life of his son. If he chose to go by the book, his son would die. Deep down, he knew not to play with their kind. He wished he could kill them all, but he couldn't. There was only one person he could take it out on. Elan.

* * *

"El Moreno," Chavez yelled.

I was sleeping hard. I got up quickly and reached for the gun under my pillow. I looked up to see Chavez standing by the bed laughing.

"Wake up, today we go to L.A."

I laid my head back in the pillow. After an hour, I came down the stairs. I found Meno and Chavez in the kitchen talking. They were whispering something to each other. Chavez nodded his head as Meno spoke. When they saw me, they stopped.

Affiliated II

"Señor Ty, Rebecca, said you like my toys, huh?" Meno said.

"Yeah, I took one out for a while, the SLR is real mean," I said.

"Yes, yes," Meno said, patting me on the back, "Chavez, will take you to Los Angeles, and you will meet some more of our friends. While you're there, stop by Icon at Playa Vista, my Villa. You can remain there until this situation has been taken care of." Meno handed me a set of keys. "If you like the toys here, wait till you see the ones of mine in L.A.!"

I took the set of keys and went up to pack my things. There was an envelope sitting on my bed. I opened it and pulled out several stacks of hundred dollar bills. It probably was about a hundred grand. Some fuck off change. This wasn't shit for L.A. though. But I was just going to chill, not kick it anyway.

Arriving in L.A.X. was a relief. Shit! I was gon' be able to breath a bit now. Chavez and I were picked up by a custom Escalade. We sat inside the SUV behind a divider that separated us from the driver. It had a pop up 42-inch plasma on the divider, the kind of airplane seats that lay all the way back, a computer, and a satellite for television.

"This is mine," Chavez said calmly. Chavez was out of L.A. He told me how he had been sent to be a representative for the Sinaloa Cartel, because of his college education. He'd majored in psychology, technical engineering, and liberal arts. The Cartels needed him. El Chapo needed him. He instructed me on which hoods I could go in, and which hoods were off limits. Due to the gang territory, a lot of areas I wanted to check out was off limits to me. You really had to be plugged in with someone.

We went to Chavez's home. He stayed in Crystal Cove, in the hills of Newport Coast, in Newport Beach, CA. It was a Spanish Colonial Estate by the seaside. Chavez ran upstairs, then came back down shortly. I looked around at the luxury that was his home, versus the shit in Meno's. Chavez was a modern type guy. Meno was very traditional, in Mexican décor. Chavez had the latest of everything. He gave me a brief tour, then we left. We were to meet the others at Ruth's Chris Steakhouse, a restaurant in Beverly Hills.

When we arrived at the restaurant, Chavez looked at me. "Señor, do not stare at anyone at the table for too long, do not talk unless you are spoken to. When you meet them, shake their hand and bow your head."

"What? Who the fuck is these mafuckas!?" I asked.

Chavez looked at me very seriously. "They're the heads of the Cartels."

This was no time for me to be bullshitting around. We met at Ruth's Chris because it was neutral territory and had private group dining. This was also very dangerous, because most of the men in here were wanted by the government. After hearing this, a slight nervousness shot through me. I wondered why was I here. El Chapo wanted me to dust off his nephew. I had to ask.

"The nephew in here?" I asked.

Chavez looked at me before he opened his door. "Si," he said, then he got out.

We went inside, and walked to the back of the restaurant where they were sitting. The guards stood up as we entered, the heads stayed seated. They didn't look surprised; they knew I would be here. Chavez walked around individually greeting everyone. I looked around and noticed one of the men staring at me. He was much younger than the others. He must've been El Chapo's nephew. I started to greet them. When I got to him, he looked at me and stood up.

"You with my uncle?" he asked with a stare, like he was trying to look into my soul. He was very young to be so serious. I recognized his dangerous looks and demeanor. It must have run in the family.

I didn't say anything. I didn't know it was a question at first. I thought he was just saying he knew about me. Chavez looked at me and nodded. I started to feel like this was a life or death question. Everyone looked at me for my answer.

"I'm with the family," I said.

They all sat and nodded their heads at each other.

Chavez nodded. "Gentlemen, we are here because we seek similar goals. We seek to put an end to this war and put an end to this informant. Everything is a process. We have taken the first steps to get rid of the rat, and now we must get rid the problem of the war. It will not be easy! Once it is accomplished, we will have someone that is more logical and less complicated."

One of the heads looked at the others.

"How would we trust that Meno will be perfect to head the Sinaloa, how do we know he is reliable enough?" he said.

El Chapo's nephew spoke up. "I have spoken with Meno on several occasions, he is a good man."

"What do you know? You're still young, what have you proved?" another interrupted.

The nephew didn't speak; he knew it wasn't time to argue.

"Look," Chavez said. "Meno is from Sinaloa, so there will not be anyone to head the Cartel unless they are from there."

"So far from what I see, Sinaloa produces rats, look at Elan!" one of the heads shouted.

"Calm down," the nephew hissed in a low tone.

The man looked in the youngster eyes. He didn't want to create a scene, so he sat back in his seat.

"One man has never acted on behalf of a whole Cartel, so watch what you say, and who you are calling a rat," Chavez said. "Now, Meno is ready, and once the problem is solved, he will be meeting with you all." He nodded his head, "Enjoy." He got up, looked at me.

I got up, and we both walked out. The nephew came out behind us. The heads were smoking cigars and drinking, laughing like it wasn't just a serious situation. I watched as the nephew walked up.

"El Moreno, Chavez spoke highly of you, homie," he said. "We gotta sit down, we'll talk later." He looked at me, then at Chavez. He walked back to the private booth.

I really wanted to know what the fuck was going on, but I waited until we got in the ride.

"What the fuck is up!?" I said. I was tired of the bullshit political beef and not knowing what was going on.

Chavez looked at me, then leaned his seat back. "You heard every word. The Cartels are getting restless. El Chapo has disrespected everyone and can no longer head the Sinaloa. Meno will step in, and that will be to your advantage, since you two are so close. Although El Chapo is ruthless, he understands someone will step in to claim his stake. That's why he is forcing you to kill his nephew. His nephew is the only one who is bringing a considerable agreement to the table to end the war. El Chapo thinks he can take on all of the Cartels. He is stubborn, and he has too much greed, so he must go!" Chavez looked into his rearview mirror. He watched as the heads left the restaurant and got into their cars. "Señor, you only see the U.S. side, not Mexico. A war is going on constantly. Bombings, senseless murders of families to send out messages, agents dying. North America is nothing but a slick talking drug addict, and we are the dealers. You want to do business with this addict, then get rid of his supplier," Chavez said, pulling off. He dropped me off at Meno's Villa. It was just yards away from the Pacific Ocean.

"How long I gotta be here?" I asked. I wanted to know because if it would be awhile, I needed some change. L.A. was expensive, especially the part I was in.

"Just a little while," Chavez said.

"I'mma need some change," I said.

"I'll have someone bring a new I.D. and a card to you tonight, you can use that until you leave," Chavez said.

I got out the car and grabbed my things, and he pulled off. The Villa was a sleek tri-level home. I went inside and dropped the bags at the door. The furniture was updated and made it look like a model home. The dining room was laid out with plates and utensils already set on the table. It looked like someone had just got through cleaning. I put my things away in the bedroom and laid on the bed. "Meno being the head of Sinaloa," I thought, "damn. I'll be a billionaire by forty." That was too sweet for me, I knew it was time to be real careful, even more than before, because things were about to get worse.

Chapter Eleven

Shai sat flicking through the channels. She had been keeping up with the war. And she'd heard about the informant. She couldn't reach Meno, but she knew he'd have no calls coming in right now. It was best that she kept their number alive until he notified her. She was bored of sitting around in the house. Going out with Moni and Kristy even got old. They were right, but she didn't just need some, she needed someone to talk to. She looked at the card that Skills dropped in her purse. She had set it on the end table and contemplated on using it. She read the card: Kaleed Moore, Pinnacle Realty.

She dialed the cell phone, and it rang, then went to voicemail. She left a brief message and a call back number, then hung up. She was bored and really wanted to get out and do something. She didn't want to go to sleep, she didn't like the dreams she was having. The phone rang, she answered it.

"Hello?"

"Yeah, did someone call this number?" Skills asked in a proper tone.

"Yeah, this Shai," she said. "You sound all proper and shit."

"That's my business tone, what up? I didn't think you was gon' call me. I thought I was gon' have to pay Kristy to set us up on a date or something," Skill said as he laughed.

Shai didn't comment on what he said. She really wished she hadn't made the call. She wanted Ty back.

"Well, what's up?" Shai said instead.

"Nothing. Trying to see what up wit you," Skills said. "Why don't we meet somewhere, let me come and scoop you?"

"Naw, I'll meet you somewhere though," Shai said. She wasn't about to let nobody know where she stayed.

"A'ight then, we can meet at Moe's Seafood, downtown in about two hours," he said. "That's cool?"

"Yeah, I'll be there," Shai said, then she hung up the phone.

She didn't really get dressed up for this little rendezvous. She wasn't interested, just wanted to do something different. She waited outside Moe's in the ride until he called. She went inside and found him sitting at a booth. She slid in, wearing a Prada jump suit.

Skills was no comparison to Ty. He was cute, but Ty's aura alone could dominate Skills. He had a little style though. East Coast flavor style that Shai had to get used to. She'd grown up in the Midwest, and there was certain shit that they just didn't rock. Skills was dressed in a designer t-shirt, a sleeveless hoodie, and some blue jeans, with some Timberlands on. He had a nice size earring in his ear, along with a long platinum chain with an emblem on it. The emblem was all diamonds and rubies in the shape of a bent spoon. Shai stared at the charm.

"What the fuck is that?" she asked.

"This?" He held up the charm. The spoon was all white diamonds and the yellow diamonds and red rubies looked like fire under the spoon. "This my logo."

"Your logo?" she asked.

"Yeah, my logo," he said, dropping it back down to his chest.

"So what's up?" he asked.

"Nothing, trying to get the feel of East Coast living," Shai said. "Shit out here is crazy."

"Where you from?" Skills asked, picking up the menu.

"I'm from out West," she said. She didn't want to give him any truth to her at all. She didn't want to get attached to anyone.

"Out West?" Skills replied. He had already asked Kristy about Shai, and she said Shai was from St. Louis. "Damn, why you out here?" he asked.

The waiter came over and sat drinks on the table, then took their order.

"Just wanted to change the scenery," Shai said.

"Damn, it's a recession, and you got it like that, huh?" he said.

"So, what's up with you and ya frontin-ass realty business?" Shai asked.

"Damn, Ma! I might have to feel them titties and see if it's a wire in there," he said.

"You the one got the spoon on ya neck, promoting. And it ain't realty," she said, smiling with a sarcastic grin.

"So, what you do?" he asked.

Shai thought about it, what did she do. She didn't do shit! Just collected.

"I'm a consultant," she said.

"Consultant for what?" he asked.

"For whatever you do," she said.

"Realty?" he asked.

"Nope," she said, taking a sip of her water.

He looked at her and grinned. "What you do? You mule shit?" he said.

"What? Nigga, please," she said. "You don't even know."

His expression went from grinning to a serious look. "You wanna know what I do, let's finish eating, and I'll show you," he said. They ate without much conversation. Skills paid for the meal, then they walked out. Shai was on her way to her truck.

"What, you don't want to ride with me, you think I'mma do something to you?" he said.

Shai stopped. "Naw, I'm about to put my purse up." She reached into the truck and took the .25 out the stash and put it in her side where she had a little holster strapped, unnoticed. She walked back over to Skills's Benz Jeep. She got in, and as she closed the door, he reached over and grabbed her by the neck.

"Bitch, who the fuck you with, the Feds?" He ripped open her jumpsuit jacket and shirt trying to see if she was wearing a wire.

"Nigga, if you don't let me go, I'll blow yo' motherfucking nuts off," Shai said calmly. He squeezed her neck tighter, so she pressed the gun to his balls, so he could feel it. He looked down. He rose up off her slowly with both hands in the air. She didn't fault him for his actions, she could understand the paranoia. She opened the door and slid out. "I ain't gon' hold that against you. I can see where you coming from, but don't ever do that again," she said. She had to admit to herself she liked the aggressiveness. She tucked away the gun as she lifted her shirt.

"You satisfied now?" she said as she turned around.

He looked and grinned. He'd never met anyone like Shai before, and she knew that. She also knew that she could get paper out of him. Real paper.

* * *

"Bong-bong bing! Yeah, nigga," Chad said, picking up the money from the table. They had been playing video games all day. Boo was getting tired of the shit. Plus, Chad had been getting rich off Rell and Boo both, playing boxing.

"Man, what the fuck, this shit is crazy just sitting here," Boo said. "I got bills, my people got bills, shit! Soon, I'll be broke."

"Chill! Ty gon' hit us in a minute," Rell said. He wasn't sure though, he had been calling Ty's phone and getting no answer. He wanted to know what was up, too. The money was getting tight, and if they kept going like this, they would have spent a million easy.

"Check this right, I still got that plug in the Valley," Rell said.

"My nigga," Chad said. "See what up, how much we can get?" Rell grabbed his keys off the counter. "I'mma swing by the barbershop real quick and holla at Cooly, I'll be back."

* * *

I got up to the sound of someone walking in and grabbed my glock. I crept to the front door. The knob twisted slowly, and the door opened.

"Ooh, shit, don't shoot man," some white boy yelled. "Am I at the right spot?" he had a set of keys in his hands. I snatched them away.

"Where you get these?" I yelled.

"Aw, fuck man, I work for Meno, I clean up around here. Chavez gave me these to give to you. You got a serious problem, dude!" the white boy said.

I grabbed the envelope from his hand. "Give me this shit and get the fuck outta here," I said. I didn't want to be that way, but I was pissed that he was creeping in here like that. He'd scared the fuck out of me for real. I thought they was coming.

"Alright, I'm out," the boy yelled as he hurried out the door.

I opened the envelope and a new identity slid out into my hands.

"How the fuck?" I mumbled to myself, looking at the I.D. It had a picture of me on it already. My new name was Ramon Dennis. I looked through the papers and a black card fell to the floor. I picked it up and looked at it, the name on it was Ramon Dennis.

"Damn," I said. Chavez had a mean hook-up that he had to turn me on to.

I wanted to hit Rell up. I'd seen all the missed calls from him, and I didn't want to leave him out in the cold. But I couldn't just yet. I couldn't call no one. I had to just stay around until someone popped up.

I walked around the crib, then hopped in the shower, and then threw on some clothes. I went out back to the garage to see the toys Meno had out here. It was only a two car garage, so I wasn't expecting the same shit as his Phoenix residence.

I opened the garage and a Maybach 57 sat in there, along with a Lamborghini. Damn. Meno had this shit sitting around and wasn't even driving it. I took the Maybach out first, driving up Santa Monica Boulevard. I got a bite to eat at Dan Tana's. It looked like a old-fashioned hang out. They did their best disguise with the sunglasses and hats. It was a good Italian restaurant. Out of all people I saw in there, I didn't expect to see El Chapo's nephew. I felt this wasn't a coincidence. He walked over to my table. Two guards stood by the door, and some sat at other tables.

"Señor Ty, what's up? Let me join you?"

"Go ahead," I nodded. "Have a seat." I put down my utensils while sliding my plate up.

He sat at the table and took a deep breath. "Ah, L.A. You like it so far?"

"I don't know, I haven't did anything yet," I said.

"So, how's things back home in St.Louis, Señor?" he asked.

"Slow."

"Of course it is," he said. "You are in the presence of a very stubborn man."

"Who? You?" I asked.

He waved to a waiter and asked for a bottle of Tequila. "No. My uncle," he said. "How do we make money in war?" he asked.

I just shrugged my shoulders.

"We don't. We spend," he said. "My very own uncle would have you to dispose of me."

At that comment I tensed up. I felt Chavez had sold me out, that's why I was here.

El Chapo's nephew must have sensed it, because he held up a finger. "Don't feel threatened, El Moreno, I'm not here in a hostile manner. My uncle did not choose you, Chavez did. Chavez informed me that you did not want to take on the task. Like I said, my uncle is very stubborn, and I hate to have to kill him, but it must be done."

"So where do I come in?" I asked.

"You are our number one consumer, and when this is over, you will be our first born, spoiled." He took a shot of the tequila. "My vision is to merge the Sinaloa and Tijuana Cartels together. Giving the Juarez and the Gulf Cartels more territory. We will take territory of the highest consumer. The one problem is El Chapo. My uncle don't trust any of us now that this deal has been brought forth. So we can't get close enough." He poured another shot, then looked up at me. "You fear my uncle?" he asked.

"I fear no man," I said.

"Good, then there should be no hesitation when it's time." He sipped his second shot. "You take care of this problem, and you will always be in good graces with the Cartels."

I sat back in my seat. "How the fuck," I thought, "am I suppose to knock this mafucka?" Before I could speak my mind, he began to speak again.

"Chavez will take you to the airport tomorrow. You go back to St. Louis, keep the deal with my uncle, and I will contact you when I get to Chicago. I may have something for you." He got up and shook my hand. Then he whistled to the guards, and they all left.

I sat thinking about the whole situation. El Chapo was trying to play me. He wanted to send me off on some dough-boy shit. For that reason alone, when the time came, there wouldn't be no hesitation.

Chapter Twelve

Rell and Boo got the rooms at the Econo Lodge. The connect wanted them to get rooms with the outside door. They got two separate rooms, so that they could chill in one and watch the money in the other. They didn't want the money to be at the same hotel as they were, but they also didn't want to drive back and forth to get the money. One point two million sat in a bathtub in the room next door. Both of them were on pins and needles about the deal. Rell knew the last deal didn't go down like this. He wanted to pull out, but he needed this come up.

They were in McAllen, Texas, down in the Valley. What they didn't know was that they were in one of the roughest neighborhoods in the city, La Paloma. They were to wait on the connect to come over from Reynosa, Nuevo Leon, in Mexico.

Rell sat in silence. He'd told Boo to bring a burner, just in case some bullshit went down, and he was glad he had. The phone rang, and Rell answered.

"What's up?" he said. The guy on the other end of the phone told Rell that Rueben wanted them to meet him real quick at a little restaurant up the road. Rell hung up the phone and grabbed his things.

"Let's ride," he said.

"Who gone stay wit the dough?" Boo said. Boo wasn't trying to take no losses.

"They don't know exactly which hotel we at, or the room. We just running down the street real quick. They wanna holla at us." They got up and left.

A car sat across the street from the hotel. The Mexicans watched as Rell and Boo left the room. They waited until they pulled off and headed down to the restaurant, then they got out and went up to the room and kicked it in. One guy entered the room first with his gun drawn. He ran to the bathroom and open the door. "Nothing," he yelled.

"Fucking gringos," the other yelled.

Before he walked out of the room, he noticed a room key lying on the bed. He picked it up and looked at it. It was the key to next door. "Vena qui, next door," he yelled with a smile.

* * *

Boo was searching in his pockets. Rell looked at him like he was crazy.

"Nigga, what, you lost ya phone?" Well asked.

"Naw!" Boo kept searching. He didn't want to tell Rell that the key to the money room was missing.

"Well, what you looking for nigga?" Rell asked, slowing down.

"I can't find the room key to where the money at. Turn around!" Boo said. Rell busted a U-turn quickly, and punched the rental. They flew onto the hotel lot and noticed the door was already opened.

"Motherfucker," Boo yelled, hitting the dashboard. Rell stopped and got out with the pistol to his side. He ran up the stairs and walked in the room. He went and checked the bathroom, the money was gone. He tried to call the number he had to the connect, but no one answered the phone.

"Shit!" he yelled.

Boo came in and looked around.

"Come on! Ain't shit we can do, that money gone," Rell said to Boo, walking out.

* * *

Shai and Skills had been kicking it more often lately. He showed her everything. He loved her style and street sense. She still hadn't given in completely to him. He tried numerous times to hit it, but she turned him down. She still wasn't over Ty. She never talked about Ty to him, but Skills felt it was somebody that she might be tied to. They were riding around after getting a bite to eat when Skills's phone began to ring back to back.

"Let me get this," he said. He usually didn't answer the phone when they were out together. But it seemed like it was important. "Yo," he answered the phone.

Shai watched as he turned the radio down.

"What?" he yelled. "When?" he asked.

Shai knew when a mafucka said all that, some major shit just went down. He threw the phone down into the console. "Shit! Shit! Shit!"

"What's up?" Shai asked. He looked like he was in deep trouble. He pulled over and got out and started to pace around. They were riding up Baltimore Street, where most of the strip clubs were. She got out and walked around to his side of the truck and leaned on the ride. She hated to see him looking like this.

"What's up?" Shai asked again. If he didn't say anything this time, then fuck him. If he said what the problem was, she just might help him. He stopped pacing and rubbed his hands over his face.

"All my shit just got popped off," he said. "Everything! I'm dead!"

"Dead?" she thought. "What did he mean?" He might owe somebody, and if he didn't pay ,he was gonna die. She liked kicking it with him, even though she looked at him more like a good friend. She didn't want to see him down like this.

"I might be able to help you, if you tell me what's up," she said.

He looked at her like he was thinking "how the fuck can you help me." She talked like she knew what was up every time they discussed business. She'd even helped him out with ways to funnel money through accounts. He was desperate now and wanted to see, was she just talking shit or what.

"You can help me out, huh?" he chuckled. "I just lost a shipment of five keys, of that china. I owe a mafucka 350 thousand, and that ain't talking bout the other 200 thousand I'm in debt with." He paused.

Shai thought a half of ticket ain't shit. This lil nigga tripping over that shit.

"I got 350," he added, "but I aint got the two, so I can't get back on my feet."

"Five hundred thousand?" Shai said. "That's what you sweating over?" she said with a chuckle.

He looked at her like he wanted to reach over and choke her ass for that comment, but they were past that. He just chuckled at her. "Yeah, you can do better?" he asked.

"Let me make a call, and I'll see if I can help you out. But you gon' owe me too, big time, and if I don't get my money, you really gon' be dead," she smiled.

Shai got her phone out of her purse and called Meno. He didn't answer the phone at first. But the second time she called him, he answered.

"Hello," he said.

"Hey, how you been?" Shai said.

"Fine. And you?" Meno replied. He sounded happy to hear from her.

"I'm doing good. I'm out East, you know, where Moni's family lives. I want to get something going for myself."

"You know this is a very difficult time," Meno said. "I wish you could come, but you can't right now."

"I need something different, your friend in Chicago," Shai said. She knew he would know what she was talking about, because he'd had her get something from up there once before, and it was China white.

"Please, I need this," she said.

Meno didn't speak.

Shai knew whenever he paused like this on the phone, he was going to give in.

"I will have someone contact you, not by this number though. Give me another number to reach you on. Do not get it yourself, have someone else do it for you. This is not over, so you must still stay under the radar." He paused, then whispered, "I love you. Be safe!"

She gave him Skills's number and hung up. She turned to Skills.

"Someone will call you later, then you are on your own. One thing I want to know. Whoever you are dealing with now, it's done. Over. You have a new connect. These people you will be dealing with will not tolerate people who are not consistent and will punish those who do not pay by hurting their families." She hoped he took her serious, because if he didn't, and he fucked up, she would be the one who had to kill him.

* * *

Chad picked them up from the Lambert Airport. He was anticipating making some money. "What up?" he said, soon as he spotted them. He noticed the look on Boo face, it wasn't good. "Damn, what happen nigga?" Chad asked.

Boo put the bags in the trunk, shaking his head. Rell just got in the passenger seat. Boo got in the back. Chad looked at the both of them. "What happened?" Chad turned around in the driver's seat, facing Boo.

"Man, we got robbed," Boo said.

"What?" Chad said. He looked at Rell, he knew Rell would tell him the real. Losing four-hundred grand wasn't an easy pill to swallow.

"Don't look at me, let Boo tell you," Rell said. "Lets roll, nigga!"

"What's up, nigga, you gon' tell me or what?" Chad said, pulling off. Chad looked through the rearview mirror at Boo.

"Nigga, we all just took a L. I fucked up and lost the key to the room where we stashed the dough, and somebody found it," Boo said. "Shit, they was gon' rob us anyway."

"Yeah, but they wasn't gon' get the dough," said Rell.

Chad shook his head and kept driving. Rell's phone beeped twice. It was an incoming text that read: Lambert 7:30 tonight. It was from Ty. Rell was hoping that it was Ty saying he was on his way. He wanted to make up for that L they just took.

"Y'all niggas quit tripping, Ty might be on his way back tonight."

* * *

I was exhausted stepping off the plane. I rolled the luggage out the Terminal to the front. where Rell waited with Chad and Boo. They dapped me up and grabbed the bags to put them in the ride for me.

"Damn, it feels good to be back at the crib," I said. I was really lying though, because I felt fucked up for real. Soon as I landed back in da Lou, I wanted to see Shai. I started to think about her.

"Shit, I'm glad you back, nigga. I thought a nigga lost you," Rell said.

We hopped in the Conversion Van that we had together. It was all black with tint. I leaned the seat back to get comfortable.

"What's been up?" I asked.

Rell looked and shook his head. Chad and Boo did the same.

"Nigga, we just took a loss for a little over a mil," Rell said.

"What? How you do that?" I asked.

"We went down there to the Valley to holla at ya boy. Boo lost the key to the room where the money was at, and they got us," Rell said. "Plus, nigga been whispering all types of shit on the streets." Rell finished telling me about everything that had been going on. We talked about them niggas from the Mac, and what was going on with that burner case he caught. He had to pay up to fifty thousand for a fine and received probation from the state.

"Oh, yeah! I got all ya shit from the crib. The old man next door had looked out for you. He said to stop by sometimes," Rell said.

We didn't go into detail about everything that happened with Shai and Moni. We just left it alone. I told Rell what Meno told me. Rell didn't show any emotion, he'd already figured the worst.

"I'm glad you back on deck, nigga," Rell said again.

"Glad to be back. Now we can get this real paper," I said. "Niggas said we broke, huh? Chad go downtown off Broadway, we got something to pick up."

We followed the directions Chavez had given me, leading us to a warehouse in the back of Pure Passion, a sex shop right off 20th and Broadway. I took out the keys and opened the gates. The back of the building was a secluded area. We could unload all day back here. No one would ever know.

I told Chad to park by the dock, and I went inside. The warehouse was empty, it was a wide open area with six pallets sitting in the middle of the floor next to a forklift. I walked over and ripped the plastic off to check and see was if it the work. The plastic was hard, it must have been industrial, because I had to cut through it to get it to rip. Once I got it open, I looked and could see the wrapping of kilos and bales of weed. There was no sign of the heroin. I looked and saw a box sitting on the side of the bales. I picked it up and found a Trac phone in it. I looked into it and saw a number was stored in, so I called it. Someone picked up.

"This is El Moreno?" he asked.

"Who is this?" I asked back.

There was a brief silence on the other end. "Never mind who I am, is this El Moreno?" he asked again.

"Yeah," I said, walking over to the door and waving to Rell, Chad, and Boo to come in.

"What you see is all there is. The deal is one point eight." Then he hung up.

We ripped it apart and loaded it up. We had to make a few trips to get all of it out the warehouse. When we were done, we weighed it all. Any other time, I would be exhausted from weighing all of this shit, but the excitement kept us up all night. A ton of weed and a hundred bricks, at the price we getting it for, shit call me B. Pablo. Black Pablo.

Chad and Boo tossed bricks around all night. They were more excited than I was. I looked at them and realized they were the only family I had left of Shai, and now they were a strong part of our family.

"Check this out," I said, getting everyone's attention. "We gon' split this shit four ways. We in this shit together now, and ain't no getting out this shit, you in, you in! We look to make a half a mil a month apiece. That's six mil a year. They got me locked in for life, so I can't stop this shit, even if I wanted to. So remember, ain't no room for error."

Chad and Boo nodded their heads. Rell already knew what was up. We was plugged in. No way out, and no looking back. We had to die doing this shit.

"Chad, you gon' take care of unloading. Boo you gon' take care of weighing, make sure we ain't getting fucked. Rell take care of getting the paper together, and I'mma take care of distribution," I said.

We sat and discussed a few good guys who might be able to fuck wit us. Then we went to work.

The next day, I was contacted by Chavez. He gave me the number to Felix, El Chapo's nephew. He said Felix wanted me to contact him a.s.a.p. He wanted me to help him out with something. I called him soon as I hung up with Chavez.

"This must be El Moreno," he answered. "I see the 3-1-4 area code."

"Yeah, what's up?" I asked.

"I will be there tonight, I want to meet with you in person to discuss something with you," he said. "I will call you when I arrive, okay?"

"A'ight," I said. Then hung up the phone.

I didn't know what was going on, and I didn't give a fuck now that I was back on the ball. Soon as the work hit the streets, nigga started hitting. We didn't cut shit on the coke. Gave it to them raw. I was running around doing my groundwork. Seeing some old faces and getting my clientele back. I had a crew of niggas by the end of the day.

When my phone rang, I looked and had forgotten all about Felix coming to town. I was in the middle of some business and had to cut out on the nigga. I shot over to meet with him. He was at

95

the Drury Inn by the Airport. We met at the restaurant in the hotel, Lombardo's. As I approached the table, he stood up to greet me.

"El Moreno, how's it going?" he asked.

"Good, now that I'm back," I said. "How's things on your end?"

"Slow," he chuckled.

I smiled seeing that he felt how I felt in L.A.

"How can I help?" I asked.

He leaned back in his seat and twirled his drink around in his glass.

"You know with everything going on, it's hard to do business," he said. "I have some people I need to contact that I can't at this time." He took a sip of his drink and continued twirling it around in the glass. It looked as if he was trying to say the right thing. "Do you know anything about heroin, Señor?" he asked. "China White?"

"I know that it's expensive," I said. That shit was at least eighty dollars a gram. Paying anywhere from seventy thousand to one hundred thousand a kilo was crazy to me.

"Yes! Very expensive, although I have some very good friends who can reach me from where they are with a cheap price, a price that I will give to you for fifty thousand a kilo. And believe me with this, you must put five or more on it."

This shit didn't sound right to me. Why didn't he have someone he fucked with in the Chi to move it? I knew he had plugs up there. And it was just too cheap.

"Where yo profit at? You can't be making shit," I said.

"When you are in position like mine, Señor, you can rub elbows with some of the most elite drug dealers in the world. I want you to contact someone in Baltimore and distribute to them, it's a favor for a friend of ours. I will contact them, then have them contact you."

"When do I pick it up?" I asked.

"It is here already, fifty kilos." He slid a room key across the table.

I grabbed the key. We stayed and talked for a little while longer, then I left to go grab the pack. I knew all along why he didn't want to tell me the real reason behind him fucking with someone in the Chi. The Feds had to be watching him and the other Cartel leaders that was stationed in the U.S.

Chapter Thirteen

Skills hung up the phone every since Shai contacted the connect. "This bitch ain't on shit," he mumbled to himself. Story, the tall, skinny cat with the braids had warned him not to trust her. Skills just thought that was Story being vindictive, because Shai had pulled her gun out on him that night at the club.

"Man, that bitch ain't got no plug," Story said. "You know what we gone have to do."

Skills knew what Story was talking about. He didn't want to have to get down like that. Story wanted to rob the niggas from Druid Hill. He had been doing homework on them niggas and felt they was easy for a quick come up.

Skills left the room. He was getting tired of Story talking bout Shai and robbing niggas. He laid down on the bed in the next room. He knew deep down if Shai didn't come through, he was going to have no choice but to rob them niggas. If it's like that, it's like that.

Story was pissed that his man was falling for that bitch Shai. He wanted to rape that bitch and beat her ass. Then turn her out on heroine. He was that type of nigga. Soon as he got the chance, he was gonna hop on it. The phone rang on the table; Story picked it up.

"Yo," he answered. Story listened as someone on the other end said, "Call this number." The person sounding like a Latino began to call the numbers out. Story didn't have a pen, so he memorized it. Skills walked back into the room.

"Who dat?" he asked. Story held up one finger, like he was telling him to be quiet. "Nigga," Skills said as he snatched the phone.

"Damn, yo, they just gave me the number," Story said.

"Hello, hello," Skills said into the phone. "Who was it?"

"I don't know! They just called and gave you this number," Story said. He took out his phone and dialed the number into it. Skills looked at it and redialed it into his phone. He pushed send, and hoped it was the connect he had been waiting on.

* * *

I was hollering at my nigga Fats, when the phone rang. I didn't recognize the number, so I didn't answer. Then they called back again, so I picked it up this time. "Hello," I said, disguising my voice a little.

"Yo, this is Skills, out of Baltimore. I was told to hit you up."

I thought to myself who the fuck. "Oh, what up?" I said, remembering this had to be the dude that Felix wanted me to fuck wit.

"Trying to see," Skills said.

"This how we gon' rock, fly into St. Louis tomorrow, and we'll talk. Call me when you land," I said.

"A'ight, yo, I'm there," he said.

* * *

Skills hung up the phone. "Yo, that sounded like a nigga, dog."

"What he say?" Story asked.

"I fly out to St. Louis tomorrow," Skills said.

"St. Louis?" Story said. He wondered what was in St. Louis.

"Yeah, nigga," Skills said, excited that he finally got in contact. "Let me call this bitch," he said to himself. He dialed Shai number. "What up, they hit me up. I fly out tomorrow," he said.

Shai didn't say anything.

"You hear me?" he asked.

"Yeah, listen don't let them know who helped you out, and I don't want to know anything," she said. She knew the situation with Elan was still brewing, and she didn't want to put her name out there. She had already advised him that no matter what, her ticket was a hundred stacks a month for the hook up. Skills had no problem with that, because he planned on making Shai his bitch. He needed a chick like her, she'd proved to be trustworthy and down.

* * *

El Chapo paced around, twirling two silver balls in his hands. He was interrogating every worker in his fields. He wanted to know who was the one behind switching his loads. A young woman and child sat on the sofa, scared. They both knew being in his presence was very dangerous.

"Someone will tell me who," El Chapo yelled, grabbing the woman by her hair.

The child screamed.

Affiliated II

The woman's lips quivered as she spoke to El Chapo. "Por favor, Señor Chapo, por favor fue Chavez el que cambio la mota," she said.

El Chapo released her. He looked up at one of his guards.

"Get her out of here, and find Chavez for me," he yelled. He knew if Chavez was responsible, then he could be working for the other Cartels. He sat down on the sofa, twirling the stress balls in his hands. "Rats," he whispered.

Chavez left out of Valentino Disco as soon as he got the call. He headed back to the compound. Nothing was suspicious, until he pulled up. He saw a couple of guards standing out front, which was unusual. When he walked in, he saw another guard dragging the bodies of a woman and child out the back door. He didn't recognize her. He kept on to the study area where El Chapo waited. He opened the doors. El Chapo stood smiling along with a couple guards, who were armed. Chavez suspected he would have to go after somebody by the looks of the guards.

"Señor Chapo," Chavez greeted.

El Chapo shook his hand.

"Chavez have a seat," he said. "Someone has been switching my loads, and I want you to find out who it is. I suspect there is a rat out in the fields that may be working for the other Cartels." He was looking at Chavez for any signs of nervousness.

Chavez did not show any signs at all. He sat there and took the orders like he normally would.

"I will do that by tonight. You will have your rat," Chavez said.

El Chapo looked at Chavez. His hated that he wasn't man enough to tell him the truth.

"I think I will have my rat sooner than that," El Chapo said, looking at both of the guards. They walked up behind Chavez and grabbed him. One grabbed him by the neck, choking him, while the other grabbed his weapon from his waist.

El Chapo looked on as the guard choked him until he was unconscious.

"Take him out back and get my machete," he yelled. They carried him out to the building with the hole in the wall. He was cuffed to the wall, and they put his head in the hole. El Chapo walked in the room with the machete in his hand. He stepped over to the hole. Chavez was still unconscious, with his head lying through in the hole. El Chapo slid the sharp blade along the back of his neck and blood leaked down onto the floor.

Chavez awoke, lifting his head to the sharpness of the blade. He stopped when he realized where he was and what was on his neck. He tried to pull his head out of the hole, but he was trapped by a metal bar running along his back.

"I trusted you, Chavez. You have been very disloyal to me. I wonder how long and how much?" El Chapo said. "Tell me about the Cartels, and I will spare your family."

Chavez knew that was a lie. He figured his family to be dead already. He didn't say anything.

El Chapo nodded to one of the guards. The guard walked over and hit Chavez with a combination of blows. Blood ran from his mouth and nose.

El Chapo grabbed his face and lifted his head up. "You tell me, or I'll cut off your son's soccer legs," El Chapo yelled.

Chavez spit in his face.

El Chapo wiped it away, then lifted the machete to Chavez's face, and in one swift swing, Chavez's body went lifeless.

* * *

Skills asked Shai to drop him off at the Airport. She didn't want to at first, but after he practically begged her, she did. The whole time she warned him not to mention her name, or not to run off. She told him these were very serious people he was now dealing with.

He really thought she was over exaggerating about the connect. He didn't think a female point of view mattered. He thought she had probably seen them beat somebody's ass and figured they was not the ones to fuck with. Skills got out and walked into the airport.

Shai watched as he walked inside. She hoped this wasn't a mistake. She would hate to have to kill Skills.

Shai pulled off. She got a text from Moni, saying she was looking for Kristy. Kristy had taken one of Moni's Louie bags again and had never brought it back. Moni had told Shai about Kristy's ways. Shai could tell Kristy was a bit jealous, but now it was getting out of hand.

Chapter Fourteen

"Aw, shit," Story moaned. He sat in the driver's seat of Skills's Benz truck. Kristy was leaned over, sucking his dick. She ran her lips up and down the bottom of his dick. She started to deep throat him, until he came in her mouth. "Damn," he said. "That's why Skills used to sneak off wit you all the time."

"Shut up! Where's my money?" she said, wiping her mouth and holding out her other hand. Story reached into his pocket and gave her a couple of hundred. She use to suck and fuck Skills for a little trick money, but lately, Skills had been chasing after Shai. Kristy felt that Shai was cutting in on her hustle.

"Skills don't fuck with me like that. Now that Shai's around, he chasing after that bitch," she said. "It's all good though, I'mma get mine regardless."

Story saw this as a perfect moment to get someone to help him get Shai back for what she did to him.

"A mafucka should turn her ass out," he spoke out loud.

"Hell, yeah! She think she's the shit," Kristy said, still babbling on. Kristy finally answered her phone, it had been ringing the whole time she was sucking Story off. She saw it was Moni and held up a finger to Story to be quiet. "What's up?" she answered.

"Where's my shit, Kristy?" Moni asked.

"Oh! I forgot to bring it back over, here I come," Kristy said.

"Bring my shit, and stop getting my things without telling me," Moni yelled, then hung up on her.

"Fucking bitch," Kristy whispered to herself. "I gotta go," she said to Story. She got out the ride and hopped in her whip, then drove off.

Story watched as she rode off. When she hit the corner, a thought hit him, "she bout to go over to they crib." He raised up in the seat, started the truck up, and followed her.

* * *

"You want me to open up a soup kitchen, nigga?" Rell said. He was referring to a spot that bump all heroine. "I ain't got time for that shit," he said. We both knew how time-consuing heroin was. The user needed it, and that attracted too much attention. We constantly would have to move around. Out of fifty kilos of china white, I decided I was gon' hit the nigga from Baltimore with twenty of 'em, and the rest of them, I didn't know what I was gon' do. I knew a couple of people who fucked with the shit, but not on a kilo level.

"I gotta shoot down to Mt. Vernon tonight," I said. I remembered my nigga C-Bow got down on that tar. I didn't know he fucked around with the china, though. "A'ight put this shit up, and I'mma try to find out where that nigga be at."

Rell took the bricks of heroin and put it in the spot with the rest of the kilos. They were wrapped the same, except they had different tape on them. If you looked at them, you could tell the difference.

I hit the East Side, rolling through the Southend, an area on the south end of East St. Louis, over in Illinois. He stayed close to the John D. Shields housing projects. This was a fucked up hood to be in if you wasn't from here or wasn't plugged with somebody in the area. Niggas out here would rob yo' ass in front of the police.

I bent a block on Bond Avenue and saw him coming out the corner store.

"What up, nigga," I yelled out the window. I knew a lot of niggas from this hood. I used to go to the local high school. Niggas was watching me still. I could see a couple of young niggas on the corner, gooned out.

"What up, boy?" C-Bow said, throwing his hands up. "Where ya been, my nigga!?"

I got out and walked over to the corner. I put the P-89 ruger in my pocket, so that niggas would see that I was strapped and for easy access, just in case something popped off.

"Shit! Chillin, what it do?" I asked.

"Man! Ya know, trying to make the chedda better." C-Bow moved his hands a lot like a pimp would when he spoke. "Shit, lookout like a family cook out," he said. He liked to talk like one also. He reminded me of my nigga, Pimpin Tez.

"Where Pimpin at?" I asked. We all used to hang out back in the day.

"You know, probably in traffic somewhere, what up?" he said.

"Shit! Might have a lick for you, I got that white," I said.

"Ooh!"he said, grabbing his chest, "that's my heartbeat, I'm pumping that all day."

"I'mma get at you in a minute, gotta see what this one nigga gon' do," I said.

He gave me his number and told me to hit him up.

"Hit me soon as you can for sho, I need that," he said.

"I got you" I said, getting into my ride. I picked the phone up out of the console. Skills had been hitting me up all the while I was talking to C-Bow. I hit him back to let him know I was on my way.

* * *

Rell loaded up the whip. He was in an '02 Suburban. It was a mule ride. There was an airtight compartment put inside for money and dope. It was undetectable by a K-9 or a cop. He didn't notice the kilo of heroin sitting in the compartment with the rest of the coke. He had mistakenly put one in there. Chad and Boo had mixed them up earlier when they came and grabbed some work.

Kimberly was sitting in the drivers seat of the Suburban. She strapped herself in and was ready to go. This was easy money for her. Driving just a couple of hours for two g's? She was game. She was from the southside of St. Louis. Rell had met her in a club one night, and they fucked a couple of times. She seemed down, so Rell decided to find out. Plus, her apartment over on the south was fucked up. Instead of tricking on her, he would just let her earn her own cash. He closed the compartment, and she drove off. To make sure she was trustworthy, he would only be minutes behind her.

* * *

I pulled up to the airport. Skills was seated on a bench waiting out front. He got up when he saw the Maserati on twenty-fours roll by. I looked at him, and he nodded his head, "What's up? You Skills?" I asked.

"Yeah! What up?" he said.

"Come on," I said.

He got in and we drove off.

"So, whats poppin?" he said. I pointed to the dash of the car.

"I don't talk in cars homie," I said.

"Cool," he said, leaning back in the seat.

We rode quiet for a minute, but he broke the silence. "Damn, this mafucka tough, yo!" He looked around at the interior of the ride. "How much one of these hit you fo?"

"Bout a buck," I said.

"A buck," Skills repeated nodding his head.

We pulled up at the Residence Inn, off Jefferson Avenue downtown. He got a room and came right back out. We went downtown to Mike Shannon's to grab a bite to eat and discuss some business. I didn't know what he was expecting me to give him, so I just threw a number out there.

"I'mma throw you twenty bricks, that's cool?" I said.

He looked kind of surprised at first, then nodded his head. I could tell he was thinking about something. "What's up?" I asked.

"Naw, yo! You know I'm popped right, I ain't got the change. I just took a loss," he said.

"Don't worry bout dat, what you usually get it for?" I asked.

"Bout seventy," he said.

I wanted to just dump all of it on him. I didn't want to deal with it for real. I had to see if I could trust him first.

"I'mma do it for the sixty first," I said. "After this time, come with the seventy. You got a address, if not, then you got to kick it here for a couple of days until I get it there. You fuck with weed?" I asked.

"Yeah! That shit go," he said.

"Cool, I'mma give you five hundred pounds of some good green for the six hundred," I said. I called down to Meno and had another load of weed sent. Then hooked it up so that the driver would swing it out to Baltimore. It felt good to utilize the connects. I felt untouchable and deadly.

"Good looking, yo, straight up. What they call you?" he asked.

I definitely wasn't bout to give this nigga my name. I didn't know who the fuck he was for real, just had to deal with him for Felix.

"B" I said. "B Pablo."

* * *

Rell pulled up on Murda Avenue. Geezy, Tra, and Freaky G stood on the porch. They watched as he pulled the Suburban in the driveway. He unloaded the bricks, then went inside.

"Look! It's ten bricks in here, eighteen a piece. Hit me when y'all get that scratch," Rell said. He left right back out. Murda Avenue was popping with feigns all down the block. It was wide open. Geezy and them hustled like it was the 80s. Rell left the Suburban behind for them to drive it back with the money in the compartment.

* * *

Freaky G blasted the music in the Xbox. "I get it on tha low, don't let nobody know you got the shit from Yo," the music from Yo Gotti blasted in the T.V. "Nigga turn that shit down some," Geezy said, grabbing a bowl out of the cabinet. "Here do something, nigga!"

They started to whip up a brick. Tra P grabbed one of the bricks and broke it down to sell powder packs. He grabbed the brick of china. He started to bag up the packs when he noticed it smelled different from the rest. He walked out to the front porch where a bunch of smokers stood out, some waiting on them to open shop, the others looking out hoping they would throw them something for watching the block.

"Hey, Low-Low," Tra P called out to a smoker. "Come here and test this shit for me. I need you to snort this line for me."

Tra walked in the house and put a line on the table. The smoker looked at the line.

"Come on man put a little mo on there," he begged.

"Nigga just test it for me," Tra P yelled, smacking the fein in the back of the head. He snorted up the line.

"Damn," he said right after he snorted it. He leaned against the table. "Damn," he said again. Low-Low walked over to the couch and sat down. He was out in seconds. Tra watched him trip off the line. He looked at Geezy.

"It must be some killa!"

Chapter Fifteen

Downtown on the Landing was crunk. The crowd was outside of the club. I crept slowly along the brick road, so I wouldn't fuck my rims up. I was in the Maserati. Everyone was looking at my plates, and I could hear them whispering "B Pablo." Niggas knew what it meant. I stopped down in front of Fat Tuesdays and waited for Chad to come through. He pulled up shortly. He had a ride full of bitches. Skills leaned up in the whip to see the hoes Chad had in the car.

"Damn, who that?" he asked.

Chad got out and ran up to the whip. I got out to holla at him real quick.

"I need you to do something for me, real quick," I said.

He didn't say anything, just looked on.

"Take this number and call my dude, his name C-Bow. Take him five of the bricks with the narrow tape on them," I said. "That's that china, heroin."

"When you get some of that shit?" Chad asked.

"The other day," I said. "Right now, I gotta deal with this nigga from out East. The connect want me to fuck with him, so I'm on babysitting."

"A'ight, I think Boo mixed some of that shit up with the rest of the bricks last night," Chad said.

"It's all good, you can tell the difference when you look at them," I said. "Make sure you get up with dude for me." I walked back to my ride.

Chad dapped me up then walked back to the whip. He got in with the bitches, and they were looking like they wanted to get an orgy going. Skills was waving at them and trying to get one of them to come over to the ride. We had business to take care of though. I wasn't really in the mood to babysit a mafucka.

"You ain't bring no luggage did you?" I asked.

"Naw! Yo, I ain't know how long a nigga was gon' be," he said.

I looked at him. "This on me homie," I said. We pulled up downtown at the Penthouse I had just got. It was off 10th and Olive, at the Syndicate Trust Building. It came fully furnished. A tri-level apartment, with all the amenities available. Two fireplaces, a kitchen with an island, walk-in closets, a Jacuzzi bath, and a jet setter shower. It was something for the time being, until I was able to get another crib. I changed clothes, putting on my normal attire. The Prada boots, jeans and a sweater. I slid the AP on, and a trillion-cut, 3-carat, blue earring. As I closed the watch winding box, I looked at the twin Piguet watches I'd bought for Shai birthday. I thought about her and a slight depression came upon me. I had to get rid of them, but I wasn't bout to give them to another bitch. I came down the steps into the living area. Skills was sitting, peeping the decoration.

"That's real slick right there," he said, getting a glance of the watch. "What's that?"

"It's a Audemar Piguet," I said. "A little over a half a mil."

"Damn, that's that Hova shit right there," he said. I had to get him some clothes. I took him out to Frontenac Plaza. We went to Saks to go shopping. He picked out the same style of shit that I had on. I could tell this nigga was digging the swag. When I pulled out the Black Card, he was stuck. I could tell he ain't never seen no shit like this before. He was really bout to get gassed up when he see what I had to pick up. I had been keeping this a secret. I ordered it the other day and just my luck, they had one already on the floor.

I was going to get him some pieces, because the pieces of jewelry he had on was looking like mall shit. I took him to Zack, a dude I used to fuck wit on the jewelry before I started getting the real shit. Zack could get you some decent pieces. He made the chain for Nelly when he first got on. That number one chain.

I had to speed out to Arnage Road, to the Maserati/Bentley Dealership. They had called me several times, telling me that the car was ready. I pulled up, and they had the SLR sitting outside. It was black with maroon interior. I went in, signed a few papers, and one swipe of the Black Card, and I was good to go. They tossed me the keys, and I hopped in. Skills was leaning in the window, looking around.

"Hey, follow me back downtown to the crib, so I can drop off the whip. We rolling in this tonight," I said. The custom rims sat real well on the SLR, twenty-twos on the back, and twenties on the front. I dropped the Maserati off at the Penthouse, went in to let Skills change, then we hit the town.

Everywhere we went, people looked at us like we were celebrities. We got stopped by the police because they wanted to see the ride up close. I knew when I rode by the clubs it made niggas grip they bitches a little tighter. We had a couple of drinks at the Loft; a night club in da Lou, then we headed over to this new spot called Lure. Through the door, I seen some niggas from the Mac. I wasn't sweating it, though. I hit up Rell, Big Rod, and Boo. They texted me when they were out front. Rell came inside to check on me. I was ready to put a end to the beef we had with them. I wanted to holla at them, but I really didn't want to create a scene. The niggas was mugging so much, that it seemed like they didn't want to holla. I waved at one of the niggas to come over. When I did that, several of them followed behind.

"What up?" Rell asked, pulling out the gun he had.

"Naw, hell naw! Not in here. We gone holla at these niggas, if they ain't trying to rap then, fuck em," I said.

They approached where we were sitting. Skills seen the group of niggas and backed up.

"What up, nigga," one of the dudes said. He was a clean cut dude with hair like Easy's, the Lil Wayne type. He looked like he was running things over on the Mac now.

"What up," I said. "We need to holla, in private."

He looked back at his crew. They walked back towards the bar area. I walked away from Skills. "Y'all mugging too hard every time y'all see one of my niggas," I said. I was really tired of the beefing, these lil niggas didn't want to do shit.

"Nigga, that shit ain't gon' never die down, Easy was my cousin nigga," he said. "I ain't trying to rap." He walked off.

I watched him walk away. "That's the problem," I said to myself.

Rell came over.

Affiliated II

"Get them thangs ready," I finished telling him how we would handle these niggas. They looked like the type to bust on sight. Young and dumb.

* * *

"Nigga, fuck that nigga, straight up," one of the lil' young dudes said. "We knocking his ass tonight."

Easy's cousin stepped back up."That nigga talking bout let's holla, man, holla bout what?" he said. "He a straight bitch, get to the ride. When this nigga leave, it's like that."

* * *

The M.V.G. nigga sat in a ride across the street. I had Rell call them down, so if them cats from the Mac thought they were going to get something off tonight, it would go the other way. A few of them had already left out the club. I already knew that they were setting up to get at me. I wasn't sweating them though.

Skills kept asking me, "Yo, we straight?"

I got tired of him asking that shit. I could see how he felt, though. All the way down here and some shit bout to kick off, and he don't know nobody.

Rell hit me, letting me know he was ready. I got Skills, and we headed for the door. I didn't want Skills looking over at the group of niggas we was beefing with. I could see one of them on the phone, he must have been letting them know I was on my way out. I kept a keen eye on the surroundings. If a nigga was to pop out, he would catch every round from the .380 I was toting. Skills kept looking back to see if the niggas was coming.

"Don't look back, just get in the mafucking ride," I said.

He got in the whip, and I looked over at Rell. He pointed to the ride the niggas from the Mac was in. He saw them pull up and park, waiting on me. I couldn't have anything go down in front of the Lure or in this area. Cops would be on us so fast, it's crazy. That's how I knew these niggas were young and didn't give a fuck. They were ready to get down anywhere.

I hopped in the whip and took off. The SLR flew down the street like a airplane. They pulled off after me, trying to catch up, but couldn't. I could see them trying to keep a distance and at the same time keep us in their sight. Rell already knew where I was going. He got there and texted me, letting me know they were ready.

I hit up Florissant to the M.V.G. hood, then flew down Mimicka, past the alley. When the ride followed onto the street, Rell waited in the alley until they passed by, then drove out, blocking them off.

The van of M.V.G. niggas drove out in front of them and opened the van doors. Two guys hopped out with S.K.'s and opened fire on their whip.

The Mac niggas ducked down and tried to back away, but hit the truck behind them. Rell came from around the side, shooting at the ride. The car was riddled with bullets.

Skills sat in the SLR, watching. He was in shock at how it went down. He thought cops was going to swarm everywhere. He kept looking at me, as I sat calmly. Soon as the shooting stopped, I pulled out, and we all left. Except the Mac boys, of course.

Me and Skills went back down to the Penthouse. Rell came over shortly. We called Chad and Boo over and told them to bring them hoes he'd had with him earlier. When they came by, it was a party. Bitches was everywhere, sucking each other and freaking. I pulled Skills to the side.

"Hey, what happen today—" He cut me off.

"I already know the drill," he said.

"A'ight cool," I said seriously.

Rell already was at me about trusting him. He wanted to send Skills back in a box. I decided to give him the benefit of the doubt. I was hoping it wasn't a mistake.

* * *

"Get the fuck up," Geezy said, kicking Low-Low.

He didn't move at all. "Tra, what the fuck you give this nigga, get 'im outta here," Geezy yelled at Tra.

Tra came into the spot. They'd been so busy that they hadn't even noticed Low-Low lying there, dead. Freaky G looked at him.

"Cuz that nigga look dead!" Freaky said. "For real! Look! That nigga bleeding at the nose, cuz!" He pointed.

Tra bent down and found the dried up blood.

"Damn, I only gave that nigga one line," Tra said. "We gotta get this nigga outta here, help me wrap him up and dump him somewhere."

"Let's dump his ass over there with them Centralia niggas," Freaky G said.

Tra's phone started ringing. He looked at it, it was one of his customers, a white boy he dealt with from time to time. He wanted to come over and talk to him about what he gave him last night. Tra hurried and wrapped Low-Low's body up and took him out back and put him in the trunk. The white boy pulled up and came in.

"Hey," he said. "What up Geezy, Kill?" He called Freaky G "Kill" because of his last name Thrailkill. They used to go to school together. "Man, you got some more of that you gave me last night?" he asked Tra. "I fuck with that, but usually I have to travel all the way to Chicago to get it, but if you can keep it, I guarantee I can get you a lot of people who fuck around with that China," he said.

"China?" Geezy said. "China White."

"Hell yeah! That shit was some good, too, better than the shit in the Chi," the white boy said.

Tra was shaking his head and rubbing his hands together.

"Yeah, let me see if I can get some more of that. You know how to fuck with it though, cause I don't know how to fuck with it," Tra asked the white boy.

"Hell yeah! I can cut it for you so that it will still be good as hell," the white boy said.

"I'm in on this cake, nigga, don't leave me out," Geezy said.

Tra hit up Rell and explained the situation to him as best as he could over the phone. Rell told them to come up tonight, and they would work something out. The white boy left, and they went out back to take Low-Low's ass over to the area where the Centralia niggas hang. When they got there, it was some niggas hanging out on the block. So they crept around through the alley and tossed the body out behind some trash cans. They got back in the ride and pulled off. They didn't know they were being watched by one of the shorties from Centralia. He was in the window of the kitchen when they pulled up and dumped the body out. The only person he could identify was Freaky G.

Chapter Sixteen

Meno huddled down near the bed by the frightened little boy. He was being held in a house in Ciudad Juarez, Chihuahua, Mexico. It was right outside of El Paso, Texas. It was the land of the Juarez Cartel. Meno had met with them to discuss his position and the peace between them. He wanted it to all end, and this little boy's father was the key to ending it.

"Don't be afraid, little one," Meno said. "Soon as your father do what he is supposed to do, you will be home with your mother."

* * *

"You owe me on that Lakers game from yesterday," a marshal said to another. They were on duty at the witness protection for Elan. He was being held at a small house in Vail, Colorado. It was a small community, not far from Denver. Only two men were on duty, and they would rotate every other day.

Elan was asleep in the back room. He couldn't eat much, and he would stay up and yell at the Marshals all night until he passed out. A bottle of tequila sat by the bed, empty. His face was buried in the pillow. One of the Marshals open the door to check on him.

"Fucker's still breathing," he said to himself. He heard his partner yell something about the Lakers game from last night. He hurried back into the living room. "Man, fuck the Lakers! I'm tired of that damn Kobe," he said. They both looked up at the sound of a car pulling up to the house. One of the marshals hurried off the couch to the window to see who it was. He had his hand on his service weapon.

"It's Ted," he said, looking out the window. "What's he doing here?" the other guy asked. They holstered their weapons and opened the door.

Ted got out the car. He wiped the pouring sweat his face. For some reason, he couldn't stop it. All he thought about was his son. He wanted to do it by the book, but he knew his son would be good as dead. The government really didn't care about his child. They would've tried to make a deal with the Cartels. His son was no bargaining tool. He walked up to the two marshals standing on the porch of the house.

"Hey, fellas, what's going on?" Ted said.

"You tell us, we weren't expecting to see you for another week or so," one of the marshals said. "He wasn't supposed to go out today. We didn't get a transport fax."

"No, I was just stopping by to check on you guys, you know these Cartels are restless in trying to find out where this guy is at," Ted said.

"Yeah, well, come on in, we were just about to watch the game," one of them insisted.

The other marshal looked at Ted. He wasn't buying what Ted was saying. He looked at the sweat and the body posture. Everything he knew said Ted was lying.

They walked inside the house. Ted looked around, and he could see the back room door cracked. Elan's legs hung off the side of the bed. He looked at the marshals, both of their weapons were holstered. He also saw that both were wearing their vests. As they walked over and took a seat, Ted opened fire on both of the men.

One of the men hit the floor from three shots in his chest. He was balled up on the floor, holding his chest.

The other marshal dove behind the television. He tried to get out his weapon, but it was too late. He took four shots to the body also. Ted did his best to him them in the vest, he didn't want to kill them. He just wanted to wound them until his job was finished. He could hear them wheezing for breath. A puddle of blood was forming under one of the men.

He went to the back room to find Elan. Elan was standing in the corner. When he'd heard the shots, he'd jumped up. There was no where to run. The stupid-ass marshals hadn't put an escape route in the room. When he saw Ted, he thought he was safe.

"Get me out of here," he yelled to Ted.

"You mo-ther-fucker," Ted yelled. He raised his barrel and shot Elan several times in the face and chest.

He came out of the back room. One of the marshals was trying to call for a dispatcher. The other one was lying lifeless. The marshal dropped the radio when he saw Ted enter the room. He reached for his weapon. Ted was already loading in another magazine.

"Tell everyone," he cried lowering his head, "I'm sorry, the sons of bitches got my son," he cried, then fired a shot in his head.

* * *

"Nigga, you gave me that boy, and boy, it got mafuckas out here looking," Geezy said. They were at one of the spots on the East Side in Parkside, a neighborhood by the Club Casino. Fats ran the spot we were pumping in. "I need all the game on that," Geezy added.

"What y'all turned the town out on that shit?" Rell asked.

"Yep, this nigga started to mix that shit wit the coke, and mafuckas went nuts," Tra said.

"Where ol' Freaky at?" Rell asked.

"Back at the crib, I'm telling you, we can't close down shop. It's popping too hard, nigga. What's up, we need dat," Geezy said.

They had started a epidemic down in the town. Mt. Vernon, Centralia, Cambria, and Carbondale wasn't used to shit like that. Niggas had already put out threats to them for taking clientele. Some niggas from the Chi tried to come down with some of the same shit, but couldn't match the prices.

When they got back to town, Freaky G had the spot on lock. There was a line out the door. They hurried out the ride and ran inside to get some of the money. They never seen anything like this before. It was mafuckas from all over, coming to try and cop some of the shit. The mix was what they wanted.

Geezy went to get his burna out. He didn't trust all the feigns standing around the spot. He knew something was bound to happen. Just as he came back with the burna, Freaky G was chasing a mafucka out the house and down the street. Tra was laughing, because of what just happened. Geezy didn't know what had happened, so he followed in pursuit. Once they caught up with the feign, they beat his ass.

Geezy walked back in, "Nigga, why you ain't help him?" he asked.

"Who the fuck was gone watch all these mafuckas?" Tra said.

"He wouldn't even made it out the door, if you would've helped him," Geezy added.

"Nigga, the shit was funny as a mafucka. He tried to short Freaky, right, so Freaky snatched the pack back out of his hand. That nigga stole on him and broke, cuz," Tra said. "I had to laugh, you should've seen his face!" Tra pointed to Freaky G.

"Nigga, fuck you," Freaky said, walking back into the room.

* * *

The money was piling faster than I thought. I needed the loads to come quicker. I dropped Skills back off at the Airport after I got confirmation that the load had reached Baltimore. Felix was giving the same demonstration. I missed one of his calls, so I hit him back to see what he wanted. When he answered the phone, it sounded like he didn't have a care in the world.

"El Moreno, como te va, how's it going?" he said.

"I'm cool, what's up?" I asked.

"Just found out that our little friend has passed away, you haven't seen the news?" he said. If he mentioned the news, then I knew he was talking about Elan. "Have you heard from Chavez?" he added. "He should be ready for Meno to take position now."

"Naw! I haven't heard from him," I said. Him mentioning Chavez made me think I did need to contact him about that Card hook-up.

"Well take care, and I will hope to see you soon," he said, then hung up.

* * *

Skills hopped in the driver's seat of his truck. Story wanted to know what went down. Skills was just looking at him. Then Story noticed his clothes. He knew that wasn't Skills's style of clothing.

"Nigga, what the fuck you got on, yo?" he asked, laughing at the outfit.

"I know this shit is fly, right?" Skills said.

"Hell, naw, nigga. That ain't how we rock," Story said. "I'mma stick with the Timbs. So what's up, we straight?" he asked.

Skills looked at him. "Nigga we straight," he said, letting Story know it was official. He called the contact and got the directions to the address. They pulled up to get the work. A tall Mexican came out with the bags.

"Skills, Skills is that your name!?" he asked.

Skills nodded yes.

The Mexican invited them in and put the bag on the table. He opened the bag and showed him the work. "Every month 1.7, plus my ten thousand for the trip," the Mexican said. "This one is 1.5," he added.

Skills shook hands with him. "Got you," Skills said.

Story looked on as they continued to talk. They loaded the bags in the truck, then shook on it again and left.

"You fucking with some Mexicans?" Story asked.

"Naw! Dude black," Skills said.

"Black?" Story asked, shocked to hear that a black dude would have a plug like this.

"Yeah! The nigga on yo! Call his self B Pablo, the Black Pablo," Skills said.

"B Pablo, huh!? Well, since you been kicking it with B Pablo, the Black Escobar or whatever he think he is, Arteaga said we got two weeks to get his dough," Story said, hitting the dash. "I figure we take this shit, fuck paying Escobar, get Tega his shit and get our plug back."

Skills turn towards Story; he wanted to tell him everything. He wanted to tell him that maybe Shai was right about the nigga B Pablo, he ain't to be fucked with. The way he stood on them niggas in the Club, he knew if he ran off, they was coming.

"Nigga, fuck Tega, we got that nigga dough, we'll have that in a week," Skills said, looking at Story and letting him know, end of conversation.

They got to the spot and unloaded the work. Story was still trying to convince Skills to run off with the load and hit Tega with the money. Skills was getting tired of his ass. He figured that Story might switch on him if things got to out of hand. He had to keep an eye on him.

They broke up the weed first. Then they went at the china. He hoped it was some good dope. He didn't want Story to have a reason to go on about jacking the load and running to Tega. He put a three on it and gave it to a junkie. The junkie shot it up and before he passed out he mumbled, "hell, yeah!"

Skills put a five on the rest of it and put it out there.

"Nigga, we got twenty bricks of this shit, why the fuck would I go back to a nigga that's only hitting me with ten, and taxing me," Skills said.

Story was quiet. He just shook his head, he'd always feared Tega. And when the time came, he was gon' make sure he wouldn't be the one going down.

After Skills put the dope out there to his workers, he called up Shai. He wanted to thank her, so he planned on taking her out to eat. When Shai came out the house and got in the truck, she saw what Skills had on. It immediately reminded her of Ty.

"What made you cop that shit?" she asked.

"Why, you don't like it?" he asked. "It's my new swag."

Shai just stared at him. She started to wonder who he saw, and what he had been doing. He started talking about things he was going to get.

"I'mma get that new Maserati, that mafucka is tough, yo!" he said.

She started to feel uncomfortable. A eerie feeling came over her as he continued to talk. She thought more about Ty, and began to have the feeling that he may still be alive. She didn't want that feeling, she was just getting over that emotion. If it resurfaced, and Ty wasn't anywhere to be found, then it would crush her even worse than before.

"Drop me back off," she said.

"Why? What's up?" Skills asked.

"Just drop me back off," Shai demanded as she got serious and reached into her purse to put her hand on the butt of her gun.

"A'ight, yo! It's like that, huh? I was just trying to take you out, thank you for your plug," he said.

Shai had blocked him out. She didn't want to pay any attention to him. She was weak right now and about to break down. Skills pulled back up to her ride. Shai grabbed everything in a rush. Skills watched her as she fiddled with her keys.

"What's wrong with you?" he asked.

Shai didn't say anything as she opened the door and got out.

"Who did you see?" she asked. She had to know.

Skills had a puzzled look on his face.

"Who did you go see?" she screamed.

"Tsst." Skills shook his head, he dropped the gear in drive. Shai stood firmly in the door waiting on him to answer her. "Pablo," Skills said, "Close my door."

Shai slammed the door and he pulled off.

Chapter Seventeen

Meno had Juarez, the head of his security, meet with other men from El Chapo's security. Juarez knew several of them. They were from the same area in Mexico. He invited them over to Meno's home for a meeting. Meno wanted Juarez to discuss a deal with them. Juarez was left alone with the men after he assured Meno that he could handle it.

All of the men sat on the sofas and sipped their drinks. They talked about old times, and about the events that recently took place. Juarez came back into the room. The men got quiet. He paced back and forth, then sat down in a chair. He leaned forward.

"You all know that El Chapo's at war with the Cartels. They will not back down for no one. You know soon this will only get worse." Juarez leaned back into the seat. "So here's the deal." He got out the seat. "Meno is the new boss, there is no more El Chapo. He must die. You will be taking orders from Meno now, do this, and your families will live." He could see the tension rising from the guards in the room. Almost on cue, several other guards stepped in the room, heavily armed. They wheeled in carts. The carts were covered with blankets. They looked around, they were trapped. No way out.

"There were some who were just too loyal and stubborn, like El Chapo," Juarez said, taking the covers off the carts. Bodies were stacked on them. They'd been beaten to death, and some were even disfigured. They looked at the bodies and glanced back and forth at each other. They knew if they didn't accept, they would be among the bodies on the carts. One of them nodded his head in approval. He looked at the others as they nodded.

"Good, good," Juarez said. "You will remain at his compound, remember any word of this and your families…" Juarez let the words trail off into their imaginations as he pointed towards the bodies.

* * *

Shai convinced herself that it was just a coincidence, the way Skills was dressed. She didn't want to stir up old emotions when she was just starting to deal with them. The name Pablo didn't register to her at all. She'd never heard of any one by that name. She walked across her bedroom to her closet. She opened the door and walked inside. She figured she would change into something, and her and Moni would go get a bite to eat. It looked like someone had been in there, looking around for something. Clothes had been tossed everywhere. She rummaged through her belongings and noticed that some of her things missing. She already knew who had been in her room.

"Moni," she yelled through the house. "Where the fuck is Kristy?" She was ready to fuck Kristy up.

Moni came in the room and saw the mess. Shai was missing clothes, bags, and shoes. It looked like a break-in. Moni knew Kristy has crossed the line this time. Shai was more family to her than Kristy. She also knew there would be no convincing Shai not to do anything. Shai was already in her sweats and tennis shoes, on her way out the door. Moni followed behind her as she got in the Rover.

Moni knew a couple of hangouts where Kristy might be. They went by there first and found out Kristy was down on GreenMount, at the North East Market, with a group of friends. Soon as Shai spotted her, she threw the Rover in park and hopped out, running up on her. She flew through the crowd.

"Bitch," Shai yelled, hitting Kristy with a blow to the face.

Kristy fell back into the crowd, and they pushed her back away from them. Shai grabbed her and started hitting her with blows as she held her hair. One of the girls Kristy was with tried to jump in and help Kristy, but Moni stepped in and hit her with the butt of the gun. The girl caught the blow to the mouth and fell down in shock. She held her mouth and saw the blood, then looked at Moni holding the gun. She crawled away from the commotion. Shai continued to beat Kristy's ass. Out of no where, Skills ran up and grabbed Shai off of Kristy.

"Yo, chill! You wanna go to jail?" Skills said, holding Shai back from beating on Kristy some more.

Kristy lay on the ground moving from side to side, holding her face. Story stepped up and helped her up from off the ground.

Moni grabbed Shai by the arm. "Come on, hurry up," she said, but Skills held a tighter grip.

Shai turned around looking at Skills.

"What the fuck is wrong with you?" he asked. He didn't understand Shai at all. She was too complex.

She snatched her arm away, and walked back over to the Rover. Moni waited till Shai got in, then they drove off.

Skills wondered what the fuck was going on in her mind. He knew she was going through a thang, but he didn't know what it was. He started to get curious about what was bothering her. She got to tripping over the clothes he had on the day he came back from St. Louis. Skills thought maybe her and Pablo had something going on before. That's probably why she didn't want him to mention her name. Skills walked to the Benz. He opened the door and heard Kristy screaming.

"Look what this bitch done to my face," she yelled.

Story looked at Skills as he got in the car. He knew Skills was still tripping over that bitch, even after she dissed his ass. He'd told Kristy to keep their plan a secret from Skills. He knew he was too weak for Shai.

"What the fuck was that about?" Skills asked. He looked at Story.

Story just shrugged his shoulders. "I don't know, yo," he said.

Skills looked back at Kristy, he saw blood all over his seat.

"Get the fuck out my shit," he yelled, getting back out the front and opening the back. "Come on!" He grabbed Kristy by the wrist. "Get yo mafucking ass out my shit!"

"Come on, you bugging," Story said. He knew he had to say something or Kristy might flip on him.

"What? Bugging, nigga, you can get the fuck out, too. This bitch got blood all over my shit, and you just let her sit in the back, bleeding all over my shit," Skills yelled. He was fed up with Story. He pushed Kristy out his truck and slammed the door. He still heard Story inside saying something. "Nigga get the fuck out, go with the bitch then if you that worried about her ass," he said.

Story looked at him.

"What?" Skills said.

Story knew not to try Skills, so he opened the door and got out.

"Beat yo mafucking ass," Skills mumbled under his breath, then pulled off.

* * *

I watched CNN for the report on the drug war. The government was now offering rewards for the Cartel leaders. It was getting real intense. These motherfuckers kidnapped a Federal Marshal's son in order to have him kill Elan. That was balls. I had to let Rell know that I probably would be going down to Mexico soon. I figured with Elan out the way, Chavez would call for me to take care of that business. I really didn't know why they couldn't just pop the mafucka. I called Chavez to see what was going on with the whole situation. He never answered the phone. That was odd. I just waited on him to call me back.

The phone rang, I thought it was Chavez calling back, but it was Skills. He was calling to let me know he had that change together. I told him to give me a couple of days, and I'll reach him again. For some reason, he wanted to fly in to see me. He wanted to talk about something. He seemed to be a stand up cat. He didn't break when that shit kicked off at the Lure. Although seeing them guns blow might've played a major part in him getting that money quick.

I had gotten several calls from Melanie, the chick from Phoenix. She'd left messages asking me to call her back. I wasn't feeling the relationship shit. I was strictly fuck and go. No strings attached. She asked to fly in, she wanted to see me. She was persistent, but not annoying. She would call, leave a message, then wouldn't call for another two or three days. She was a cool person to kick it with, but I didn't want to fly her in right now, maybe later.

My focus was getting this money. It was too much, I had to do something with it. I was trying to open up a club or a restaurant. I had cousins in college that I hadn't really talked to until I'd seen them recently out to eat. They said they majored in Business Management. I told them to put together a proposal and find a spot, then I'll take care of the rest. Cynthia, this real estate chick I knew, she had the game and gone with it. The houses were cheap now, so I cashed in on that. Whatever she wanted I gave it to her, she knew how to flip money. In a couple of years, Rell and me would have a couple of mil in the bank, legit.

I flicked through the channels. There wasn't shit on right now. The world of television was being taken over by reality shows. Rell came through the door. I knew it was him. He the only nigga with a key. With all this moving we been doing, me and him hadn't really had a chance to sit down and chop it up. I tried not to get to distant from my niggas, because people change.

"What up, fool?" he said, sitting a duffel on the table.

"What's that?" I asked.

"It's that cheddar from Geezy'nem and C-Bow," he said taking a seat on the couch. He was looking at me like he wanted to say something. "When you get that SLR, that mafucka right," he said.

I knew my nigga too well. That wasn't a compliment, that was more like "you trippin."

"I know you ain't drop cash on that?" he added.

"Hell, naw! The black card," I said, pulling out the card and flashing it to him. He grabbed it and looked at it.

"Ramon Dennis?" Rell mumbled the name on the card to himself. "Where mine at?" he threw the card back at me.

"I had just came up on it when I was in L.A. I'm trying to get everybody one, but I can't get in the dude that got'em," I said.

"Dude?" Rell said shaking his head. "Damn, nigga you ain't never kept nobody or nothing a secret from me before, never held shit back, we been in this shit fifty-fifty since the beginning, what's up?" Rell said, throwing his hands around. He was mad, and had every right to be. "First, you come back, and you don't tell me shit about what's been going on, then you change ya name to Black Pablo, got a black card, SLR, and fly some nigga in from Baltimore, what's up?" he asked.

I sank in the sofa, taking it all in. He was right. I hadn't been letting him in on everything. I didn't have a reason, either. Surely it was that my connect and the Mafia recognized me, not Rell. But at the end of the day, he was the nigga that put the work in. And he would for sure go to bat for a nigga.

"Man, you right, but shit, we been running around so much, this the first time we walked for real," I said, then I started to explain everything that had been going on between the Mexican Cartels, then the role they wanted me to play in getting El Chapo out of the way. He definitely wasn't with that shit. Rell no longer trusted them on that level, after that shit happen down in the Valley. I told him about Chavez, the black card, Felix, and the heroin, and what that had to do with Skills coming to town. When I told him about Elan, and what happened to him, he snapped.

"What?" he said, standing up. "And you running around here calling yo'self the Black Pablo?"

He was right. It was a reality check. Me being down there with El Chapo made me feel untouchable, when I wasn't. I was really still a low-level street dealer, no matter how big I got. My residence was still in the U.S., so I was easier to get than El Chapo was, and I wasn't making it hard for them to get to me. With a name like B. Pablo, the feds would surely look into it.

"I say we chill for a minute, slow it down," Rell said as he stood up. "Shit moving too fast."

"We can't slow it down, we just gotta watch what we do," I said. I stood up and grabbed the bag. Going back to Mexico was on my mind. Rell didn't like the plan at all. I reached in my pocket and pulled out the phone to all the connects I'd met when I was down there. "When I go down here to do this shit for the Cartels, if I don't make it back, this phone got every number to connects in Phoenix that's tied to the Cartels."

Rell looked at the phone. "Nigga, fuck that phone, you'll be back."

Chapter Eighteen

"So you say Skills does not want my business no more?" Arteaga spoke with his soft Puerto Rican accent. He was tall and slim, with curly dark hair. "He is dealing with someone else?"

Story sat at the table in a restaurant owned by Arteaga. It was on the West side of Baltimore.

"Look, I hollered at him, but he ain't tryna hear me. So I'm hollering at you. Right now he cutting you out, and me out, too," Story said. Story was pissed that Skills found another connect. He knew this would cut into his hustle. Story was from the West Side, and he had ties to Arteaga, so he gave Skills the plug. Skills always let Story holla at Tega for him. Story used to tell Arteaga what Skills said, and drop the money off to Tega. So he would take money off the top from Skills to Tega, leaving Skills with the debt. Now, with Skills fucking with this new nigga, there was no way he could get his pinch on. He was ready to take everything Skills had.

"You no worry. I want you to watch Skills while I check and see if he's dealing with any friends of mine,"Arteaga said.

"Unless you got friends in St. Louis, then he ain't dealing with nobody you know, dude call himself the Black Pablo," Story said.

"What?" Arteaga said laughing, "The Black Pablo! That sound like a drug dealing super hero." He continued on laughing.

"Yeah, he got it for the cheap, too, real good shit," Story went on.

Arteaga stopped laughing and leaned up in his seat. "Let me check on this Black Pablo, and you keep a eye on Skills, then you get back with me," Arteaga said. Arteaga looked at one of his men. "Carlos."

Carlos stepped up to Story, and gave him an envelope full of stacks. Arteaga looked at Story. "A little something for you," Arteaga said.

Story held up the envelope waving it to him, then walked out of the restaurant.

* * *

One of Felix's guards called him down to the front of the house, saying someone had pulled up and asked to see him, that it was an emergency. The guards held the visitor down while Felix came down the stairs. He did not recognize him. A guard walked up to him and whispered in his ear.

"He says he's from the Sinaloa," the guard said.

Felix wondered why the Sinaloa would stop by unannounced, and why it wasn't Chavez. Felix stepped up close to the man, he was holding a box wrapped in plastic. The man squinted his eyes as he looked at Felix. Felix resembled El Chapo a little.

"Who are you?" Felix asked in Spanish.

"I am here for El Chapo," the visitor said. He reached for the top of the lid and opened it. "He don't like rats in his home," he said, dropping the lid to the box.

The guards pulled their guns out and put them to his head. Felix looked in the box at Chavez's head. He could tell Chavez had been gone for a while now. He could hardly recognize him.

Felix smiled, he slowly slid the blade he kept on his side out into his hand. "You would be stupid enough to bring this to my home?" he said, sticking the knife into the man's stomach and twisting it. Felix held him up and pushed it deeper into him, while looking into his eyes. "My uncle will know my reply, when you don't show up," he said, pulling the knife out. He spit on him. "Get him out of here, get the others, and call El Moreno," he yelled at his guards.

* * *

"Ya'll heard one of them Centralia niggas went down for that body," Tra said. They were sitting on the porch of Freaky's crib on 17th street, in Mt. Vernon. The area was getting too hot for them. The cops was rolling by periodically, trying to bust anyone leaving from the street. A dirty detective, named Smiley, kept harassing them on the regular. They knew the Centralia niggas probably told on them.

"Fuck them niggas," Freaky said.

"You know them niggas ain't gon' take that body. They telling," Geezy said, passing the blunt to Freaky.

"There go Smiley, nigga," Tra said. Freaky cuffed the blunt and put it out on the side of the porch. Smiley sped up into the yard, and got out the car. He walked up looking around on the ground for drugs or drug paraphernalia.

"What's going on?" he said, approaching the porch.

"Man, get the fuck off my property," Freaky said.

"This ain't no property, this a place of business, ain't it? "Smiley said sarcastically. He put one foot up on the steps. "I'mma get you motherfuckers, you all going fed," he threatened.

"Get the fuck outta here with that shit," Geezy said. "If you ain't got no warrant, or we ain't got nothing, then get the fuck outta here fo' somebody beat yo ass."

Smiley knew taking him down on a comment was just going to ass to the harassing suspicion.

"Yeah," Smiley said, walking to the car. "Remember the feds. Y'all will be begging me to keep it State," he said, pulling out of the yard. He was known for harassing niggas. He was also known for playing the game the way they played it. Dirty.

* * *

Skills was waiting at Lambert Airport in St. Louis. He had been over the conversation several times in his mind. Each time, he had decided not to bring it up. He didn't know what the relationship was with them, if it was a relationship. He wanted to keep the connect. If it was a bad relationship, or she might've ran off with some dough, he didn't want to fuck up his plug for Shai. He wanted Shai, though. She looked out for him more than any nigga or family member he'd known ever could. He would just have to do his best at getting her. Even if it cost him, he would keep at it until she gave in.

* * *

"There that nigga go," I said to Rell.

We were in his Escalade. I waved to Skills, he ran over and got in.

"Yo, what up?" he said to both of us, as he hopped in the truck. I looked back and dapped him up, Rell did the same.

"This my nigga," I said, introducing Rell.

"What up yo, you was at the club that night," Skills said. He thought Rell was one of the niggas that put in work.

"What up," Rell said.

We rode on downtown to the Penthouse. My phone had been blowing up with calls from Melanie.

"Damn, who is that?" Rell asked, noticing my shit buzzing in the console several times.

"That's that bitch from Phoenix," I said, "thick as a mafucka. I ain't been fucking with her lately, so she been blowing me up. She sent me a pic the other day on the phone." I pulled the picture up and showed it to them.

"Damn, nigga that ass fat," Rell said. He passed the phone to Skills.

"Yo, that bitch like Vida," he said, "I'll be at this bitch."

"Man, fuck a bitch right now," I said.

"That's what I'll be doing, fucking that bitch right now," Rell said.

"Shit, I'm trying to get at this one bitch, but she ain't having it yo, straight no play," Skills said, he was talking about Shai. He didn't want to say her name. He didn't want to fuck things up.

"Stunt on that bitch," Rell said.

"Naw, yo! She ain't that type. This bitch act like she got all the paper. She ain't trippin off that shit," Skills said.

"You gotta show swag on a bitch, give her some priceless shit, romance that hoe," I said, thinking about the things I wanted to do with Shai. "I might have something for you to kick things off with, it's gon' cost you though."

"It's all good, I got that," Skills said.

We got back downtown, and I flopped down on the sofa. Rell was on the phone with Boo. I heard him saying something about the keys to his BMW.

Skills sat down, "Yo, I appreciate that straight up. I was able to get this one cat out the way," Skills said, reaching over to give me a shake.

"It's all good," I said.

Rell came back over. He had a blunt rolled up. "You smoke, nigga?" Rell asked Skills. He lit the blunt up and took a hit.

"Weed," Skills said.

"Yeah, what you think it is?" Rell asked, smirking at him.

"Shit, nigga be on that boat, sherm, all type of shit out our way," Skills said, grabbing the blunt and hitting it. Him and Rell started to chop it up together. I knew Rell was feeling him out.

I got up and walked into the kitchen. I decided to give Melanie a call. She answered on the first ring.

"Hello?" she said.

"What's up?" I said.

"Hey, how you doing?" she said. I knew she was trying to hide if she was angry from me not calling.

"I'm straight, how you?" I said.

"I'm cool now that you called, I tried to convince myself that you was real busy, and was going to get at me when you got a chance, but after a while I started to wonder."

"Naw! I have been busy lately, I'm cool now though. What's up?" I said.

"Nothing, just wanted to talk to you in person, that's all," she said.

I didn't like to wait on shit like that. Especially when they say they wanna holla in person.

"Just tell me what's going on," I said.

"I'm pregnant," she said.

It got quiet on the phone.

"Pregnant," I thought. I wanted to hit that bitch with the line from Cane in Menace to Society. "It ain't mine," I thought, "I had the jimmy on extra tight." But I didn't, I went back bareback. Damn! I let this bitch get me. I know she gon' try to keep it, especially after seeing me whip like that.

"You heard me?" she asked.

"Yeah, I heard you," I said. Before I could say another word, she blurted out.

"I'mma get an abortion, I know you don't want it."

I thought, "You mafuckin right I don't." I was shocked that she was cool with it. That made me respect her more, that she would see how I felt first about the mistake. She wasn't out for the money like that.

"Yeah, you right. I don't think a baby would be cool right now," I said.

"Well, I got the money. I just wanted you to know first, before I did it," she said. "Alright then." She was about to hang up the phone. I liked the way she was playing her cards.

"Hold on, why don't you come out here tonight on the Red Eye," I said.

She didn't say anything for a moment.

"Alright that's cool," she said.

"I'll hit you back shortly with the flight reservations," I said.

"Okay," she replied, then hung up. She probably thought she'd played her cards proper, but all I wanted was a shot of that pregnant pussy before she get the abortion. I came back in the room. Both of them were sunk down in the sofas from the weed.

"Hey, I'mma fly in that one bitch I was talking to y'all about tonight," I said.

"Nigga, tell her to bring some friends," Rell said.

I remembered how her friends looked that night. "Homie you ain't trying to fuck with none of her friends."

"They thick?" Rell asked.

"Yeah, they thick," I said.

"Well, tell her to bring 'em. Hell, yea,h I'm trying to fuck with them," he said. He looked at Skills, "You trying to fuck with them?"

"Hell, yeah, long as they ain't no fucked up jump offs," Skills said with a slow drag.

"A'ight, I'mma holla at her," I said.

We were out to eat when Boo called and wanted to meet us by the Loop. He said he was in the area, down the street at a clothing store called I AM. When he pulled up, he was in Rell's 760.

"Where yo shit at?" I asked.

Boo stepped up shaking his head, taking a seat.

"Man, I wrecked my shit last night, fucking with this bitch. We arguing, and she grabbed the wheel, we almost hit a mafuckin tree," he said. "Shit gon' be in the shop for a couple of days." Boo looked over at Skills and nodded his head. "What's up?"

Skills nodded back at him. I introduced him to Boo, "This Skills, he from out East. Skills, this my nigga, B."

"What up, yo," Skills said.

I looked at Boo and asked him where Chad was. I didn't mention his name out loud, even though we was kicking it with the nigga Skills, I still didn't want him knowing everybody name. Boo caught on quickly.

"I don't know. He hit me up earlier, but we ain't get up," he said. "I'm bout to go across them waters real quick though, gotta pick something up."

"A'ight, nigga, don't let that bitch in my shit," Rell yelled as Boo walked away.

We sat and chilled a little longer, watching all the women walk by, then we swung around to a few other spots. We were sitting around waiting on Melanie and her friends to fly in. They caught an early flight and surprised me with a phone call, saying they were at the Airport. We hurried to pick them up.

I got out and helped them with the bags. Her friends weren't the chicks I saw that night. Melanie saw me looking at them.

"These my girls, I work with them," she said. "This Charlene, and this is Veronica." They both looked good as hell.

Charlene was brown skinned, about 5'9" with a nice all-around shape. Nothing too small, nothing too big. Veronica, on the other hand, was nice. A yellow-bone, fine with a nice shape. She was tall, 5'11" and thick like Melanie. Rell saw her and instantly hopped on her first. They all got in. Luckily, we had enough room in the Escalade. It had third row seating, so me and Melanie got in the back.

"Go to the crib so we can put the bags up and switch rides," I said.

Rell took us downtown to the Penthouse. "How y'all get here so fast on a short notice?" I asked.

Melanie pointed to Charlene. "She's a flight attendant, we all got buddy passes."

Being around Melanie eased up a lot of tension. Tension that I didn't realize was there. Her presence just made me feel peaceful. I didn't want to get too attached, but I was feeling her already.

We arrived downtown, and they loved the Tri-level apartment. We all sat around talking and joking. I gave Skills the keys to the Maserati, I was going to drive the SLR, and Rell was going to ride in his new whip. He'd been talking about it, but he hadn't showed it yet. He said he had to get something, since I had gotten the SLR.

Veronica and Rell left to go change clothes and switch rides, and I told Skills he could use the navigation to get to Morton's Steakhouse in Clayton. It had it had nice lighting for us to dine. I took them all upstairs and showed Skills the other bedroom and bath, so Charlene could get ready, and Melanie where she could shower and change. As I was going up the stairs, Melanie playfully pushed me.

"Don't let me get into no fights with one of yo chicks out here," she joked.

"Naw! You straight. I ain't got no chicks that think they my chick," I said.

She just looked at me and poked her lips out. She went in the bathroom and turned the shower on. I laid across the bed for a minute. I was kind of tired, so I dozed off.

Affiliated II

When I woke up, she was on top of me, naked. She took my hand and put it on her ass. She was soft and firm, and my shit started to pulsate in my jeans. She felt it, and started to smile.

"Get up," I said.

She sat up over me, lifting her leg over my head, spreading her ass wide open over my face. She knew what she was doing. She bent over in doggy-style position and stayed there on the bed. She bent all the way down and lowered her back, pushing her pussy out.

I hurried and pulled out my dick, rubbed it along her lips, then slid it inside of her slowly. She was warm and wet.

She started to move her ass back and forth, sliding on my dick. Her ass bounced and jiggled so much that I couldn't control myself, like before. She was so good, that I came inside of her within a few strokes. It was something about her that made me cum fast as hell. She kept on pumping faster on my dick, it was still hard. I saw her leg jumping on the bed.

Her hands gripped the sheets tighter, and she tensed up. I got back into it, just from looking at her go. She pushed my hands off of her.

"Ooh, don't touch me," she said, pushing back harder on me. I had to keep my balance steady. She screamed loud. I knew Skills and Charlene heard her ass. I could feel her muscles tighten around my dick. She leaned forward and rolled over.

"That would get me ready for tonight," she said. "I been feigning for that dick, and I'm pregnant too! Shit!" She got up and walked off into the bathroom.

I followed behind her, wobbling from side to side, trying to hold my pants up. She wiped off my dick like she did before, then tucked it away in my jeans. I went to switch shirts, and she yelled to me, "Give me a minute."

I headed downstairs. I passed by the other bedroom, where Skills and Charlene were. The door was cracked, and she was giving Skills some head. Damn. I stepped to the side and peeked. Skills's back was to me, and I could see Charlene completely from the side. She had on nothing but a thong. Her titties was sitting firm, and she had a thick waistline. She was squatting down, going to work on Skills. He had his head in the air, with his eyes closed, enjoying his self.

My phone vibrated. I looked down to check it. When I looked back up, Charlene was looking dead at me. She was still sucking Skills off. She pulled his dick out and tongued the bottom of it, while giving me eye contact.

She put her hands on his ass and pushed him deeper in her mouth. Skills didn't even notice her telling me to come in, by waving her finger at me. I just smiled at her, and she closed her eyes, cocked her head to the side, and started to go faster.

I walked off into the living room. Damn. She looked like she had a good head on her shoulders. I might have to see what's up with that.

We got to the restaurant and waited on Rell to pull up. Minutes later, he pulled up. I couldn't tell what type of ride it was at first. The lights looked like a bunch of little small dots. He pulled up along side of me.

"What up thou," he said. He was stunting hard. Not as hard as me, but he was killing 'em. He was in an Audi R8, and it looked like a little spaceship. It was tough. Burgundy with the chrome and burgundy rims. He parked, and I looked over to Skills. I could see him out the window peeping at Rell's ride, while Charlene was peeping me.

We all had a good time, talking, eating, and joking around. Charlene cut me and Rell glances all night long. She was off the chain. I learned that Melanie was a good woman. Not too much into the street life. Devoted to her man and family. A wholesome chick. I didn't want to taint her character with my lifestyle. But she felt good to be around. Someone that let me do me, and not say shit about it. Like Shai. She reminded me of her so much, minus the problems.

After we ate, we split. Skills said he was cool, that he knew the way back downtown. Melanie wanted to drive the SLR. I was skeptical at first, then I gave in after she explained to me the paddle shifting. We all parted, heading in different directions. I really didn't want Skills rolling around by alone. But fuck it, he wanted to, so I let him.

Before he left, I showed him where the burna was. He said he wasn't bout to go nowhere but back to the crib and hit Charlene. I told him I wouldn't be long, when I said that Charlene smiled.

Chapter Nineteen

"Maybe you trippin," Moni said to Shai. Shai had explained the situation with her and Skills. How Skills had started to dress differently, in a similar style that Ty used to wear.

"Yeah, you right," Shai said. She'd thought about it hard and came to the conclusion that Meno wouldn't lie to her. That if Ty was still alive, he would have contacted her somehow. She wanted to apologize to Skills. She would wait until she saw him again. They hadn't seen Kristy since the incident. They figured she wouldn't come around anymore after that ass whooping.

"You wanna get out for a while?" Moni asked.

Shai thought about it. She'd been in the house for the past couple of days. That incident with Skills and Kristy had put her back in stress mode. She was really bothered by the memory of Ty. What she hated the most was she couldn't seek revenge for him. If she could do that, then she would put everything behind her for good.

* * *

When we got back downtown, Melanie was tired and feeling sick. She had drank some wine, knowing she was pregnant. She argued the fact that she was going to get an abortion, so it didn't matter. I helped her up the steps to the bedroom. She laid down and kept apologizing, saying that she fucked up the night.

"Naw! You ain't fuck up the night, go ahead and go to sleep," I said.

She laid there and went right to sleep.

I went back downstairs to the living room. Rell and Veronica came in shortly after that. They were laughing and joking. She asked where Melanie was, and I told her upstairs. She went up to check on her. Rell whispered to me about Charlene.

"Nigga, that bitch ready to fuck." he said.

"Why you say that?" I asked, playing stupid

"Nigga you seen the bitch all night looking at both of us," Rell said. "Where she at?" he asked.

"I don't know, I ain't seen either of them, I ain't go check the rooms though," I said. I looked up and Melanie and Veronica was coming down the stairs.

"I'm bout to run her to the nearest hospital," Veronica said. "She ain't feeling too good."

"Alright, let me get the keys," I said.

"It's okay. There's a cab downstairs," she said, heading out the door.

"Ya'll sure you don't need us to come?" Rell asked.

"Naw! We okay," Veronica replied, helping Melanie out of the door.

"I'mma call you," Melanie said, as they closed the door.

We both sat there chillin for a while, tripping off Charlene. We were anticipating her coming in the door. I decided I should check on Skills. He wasn't from here, so I wondered where he went. His phone just rang, nobody picked up, and I could hear the sound in the room. It was coming from under the pillow on the couch. Rell searched the pillows and found his phone.

"Damn, the nigga probably left his phone," he said.

I called Melanie, but she didn't answer. She probably had no reception at the hospital. I went up to my room. When I opened the door, my shit was all over the place. It looked like she had searched all through my shit. I went to the closet and found the drawers open. The drawer that I stashed some loose change in was pulled out. The money was gone. It was about a hundred stacks. I took out my key and open the jewelry safe, all my jewelry was still there. I ran downstairs to the other bedroom and found Skills, naked in the closet. He had a ball strapped in his mouth, like that S and M bondage sex shit. He was mad as fuck. I unstrapped the thing from around his mouth.

"That bitch, Charlene, nigga, she got me," he yelled.

"How the fuck did she get you cuffed and shit?" I asked.

He had cuffs on his hands, and his feet was tied. I didn't have a key to the cuffs, so I started looking around for something to use. I looked on the bed and saw the set of keys.

"That bitch was on some real freaky shit, wanting to gag me up and cuff me. I wasn't on that gag shit, but I let the bitch cuff me after I cuffed and banged her," he said, pulling his hands from around him as I uncuffed him. "She cuffed me like she was on some police shit. Singing that Lil Wayne shit." The nigga was a funny dude, and I started laughing. "That shit ain't funny yo," he said.

"Nigga, she got me too, took a hundred stacks out the room," I said.

When I said that, Skills shook his head.

"Damn, my bad, my nigga," he said. "This bitch put the ball on me, then pushed me in the closet. She texted somebody after that. I thought she hollered at some nigga," he said. He was putting on his shit when Rell came in the room.

"What the fuck happened to you?" he asked Skills.

"Them bitches got us," I said. I had already figured it out. "Melanie got a text saying it was her girl checking up on her. Then right after that, she started talking about she felt sick."

"Veronica got one, too. She said they was making sure she was okay," Rell said.

"The bitches got me for a hundred stacks," I said. "They probably on a flight right now."

Rell looked at me, shaking his head.

"Damn, the bitch got my pieces," Skills said, noticing his jewelry missing.

"Fuck it, nigga, you get that shit back," I said. I guess that bitch did play her cards well.

* * *

"El Chapo wants to meet at one of the Distribution Centers in the Valley. He owned a mansion there in Cimarron Country Club," Meno said to Felix.

"Okay, my friend and I will be ready," Felix said. "Notify El Moreno, and it will be an honor." Felix hung up the phone. He'd waited for this day patiently. It would be an honor to take from his uncle what his uncle had tried to take from him many times. His life.

* * *

In the midst of all this bullshit with Melanie, my phone rang. It was Felix. He wanted me to come down to McAllen, Texas tomorrow. I let Rell know, and he went crazy.

"Nigga, that's where that bullshit happen," he yelled. He wasn't having me going alone. Skills just sat there, watching us go back and forth over the shit. We chilled when we noticed Skills trying to figure out what we was talking about. I turned to Skills.

"Did we holla about what you wanted?" I asked.

Skills stood up. "Naw! I was just coming to fuck with you on some appreciation shit and holla about that broad," he said.

I remembered him talking about some chick playing hard to get. I had just lost a hundred stacks, so this was my chance to get that little change back. I wanted to get rid of the watches that I'd bought Shai for her birthday, so why not give them to him. I knew that would get him the pussy. If it wasn't for Melanie and her goon squad, he wouldn't have got it this sweet.

"Fuck it, I'mma look out for you," I said to him. "Come on." I waved to him to follow me upstairs. The watches cost a lot more than what she took. Fuck it, I wasn't trippin. "You owe me the hundred stacks they took for this," I said, giving him the box.

"What's this?" he asked. He opened the box and the watches sat inside looking new as the day I got them. The diamonds sparkled like no other kind. The clarity in them was flawless.

"Those are twin diamond Piaget watches, his and hers, the pair is of a kind," I said.

He looked at the watches, picking them up out of the box.

"Hell, yeah, this should do it right here," Skills said.

"Rell gon' take you to the airport, I gotta get ready. Be cool, I'll get at you when I get back," I said.

Rell looked at me before him and Skills walked out of the door.

"I'll be back, nigga, we gotta holla," Rell said. He really didn't want me to go down to the Valley. It was nothing to talk about for real. It was something I had to do, no exceptions.

* * *

Boo crept through Edgemont on the East Side. He was on his way to Tracy's crib. This chick he fucked with from time to time. She would hold shit for him and whip the wheel while he did his business. He had a text from Chad saying Rell wanted them to get up with Kimberly and make sure she ran that route to Mt. Vernon.

He sat in Tracy's driveway on 85th street, waiting on her to pull up. He hated to be out in the hood, especially in the 760 BM. He knew niggas and them boys might be out patrolling, and that would make him hot. He wanted to get in a rental, but had been on the run all day long. Boo watched as the same Cutlass hit the corner twice. He looked in the rearview as the ride hit the corner again.

He pulled out the glock that he had stashed on the side of the seat. He knew some shit was about to jump off. This was Edgemont, and niggas be on one out here.

Dame told his cousin to hit the block one more time. He peeped Boo sitting in front of Tracy's house. He had been anticipating this moment. They'd bent the block two times already.

"Nigga, you ain't on shit! Let's roll," Will, Dame's cousin, yelled at Dame.

"Nigga, you got me fucked up, roll down on this nigga. I think he up in there," Dame said. They bent the corner again, rolling slowly. Dame cocked the nine-millimeter he had. It was a cheap-ass high point. It didn't matter to him, because it didn't cost him shit to get. He rolled down the window, and Will stopped on the side of the ride. Dame tried to signal for Boo to roll down the window, but he couldn't see through the tint. Soon as he saw a little movement, he opened fire on the car.

Boo had leaned the seat all the way back. Boo started dumping back through the window. He saw the shooter slump down, trying to duck the shots. His arm was still out the window. The shooting stopped. Boo lifted up, he was hit in the hip and the leg. He looked over to the other ride and saw the driver laid back in the seat. His face was covered in blood. He looked at his gun, it was still loaded. Dame was hit, too, and he was trying to cock a bullet out the chamber of his weapon. Cheap-ass gun must have jammed up on him. He looked up at Boo limping over to the ride. Boo raised the burna and fired until it was empty. Three shots rang out before the gun stopped.

* * *

Kimberly was on her way to the trap to pick up the Suburban. She was driving her Mazda Millennium. She had been looking to get a new ride, and she liked that new BMW truck. It was little and slick. She had been smoking before she got to the trap. She knew Rell tripped off her smoking before, said if he caught her blowing again while she was suppose to pick something up, he would get rid of her. She had gotten some haze from her girl and wanted to blow one before she hit the highway. She looked up and noticed an unmarked pulling out in back of her. The ride hit the lights.

"Shit," she said. She wasn't tripping off anything. She knew it wasn't nothing on her, so she pulled over.

Smiley got out the ride and approached her car. "License and registration?" he asked.

Kimberly fumbled through the glove compartment for the papers. She got out her license and registration and gave it to him. He went back and ran a check on her. He found nothing. He had been watching the area, and seen her frequently coming from out of town, and leaving in a SUV. He walked back to the car.

"Can you step out, ma'am?" he asked.

"For what? I ain't got no warrants," she said, throwing her hands in the air.

"Just routine," he said, pulling on her door.

She opened it for him. "Racist-ass cops," she mumbled.

"Step over here, please," he said. "Do you mind if I search the vehicle? There are no drugs or weapons or anything inside, are there?" he asked.

"Naw, why you wanna search the car?" she asked.

He looked at her eyes and could see her pupils looked like she was intoxicated. He felt he could use that to his advantage.

"I smelled marijuana. Now, I could get the dog and let him run around the vehicle, but if I gotta go through that trouble, somebody is going to jail," he said.

Kimberly thought about it, it wasn't nothing in the ride, she was sure of it. She let him search the vehicle.

"Go ahead," she said, waving her hand at him.

He sat her in the back of the unmarked car, put on his gloves, and started to search her car. Kimberly watched as he tore up her car. He went in the backseats, then the front. Her little Mazda was destroyed. She lowered her head. When she rose back up, he was walking to the car with a small bag in his hand. He opened the door and let her out. He turned her around and started to read her the rights.

"Hold on, what the fuck is you doing?" She yelled. "I didn't do nothing!"

"I found this when searching your car," he said, flipping over a bag of crack cocaine. It looked like an ounce. "That's five to ten years right there."

"That's ain't mine, you put that shit there!" She yelled and jerked, trying to get loose.

"Calm down, calm down, you need to tell me what's going on with the SUV, and on 17th street," he said. "I might be able to help you."

"Fuck you, mafucka, fuck you, you trying to set me up!"

"Yeah, well that's what you gon' be ready to do to try to get out of this one, fuck me," he said, putting her inside the patrol car.

Chapter Twenty

I couldn't talk Rell out of coming with me. He wasn't trying to hear it at all. We were on the plane for a couple of hours before the plane started to drop out the clouds. From the window, I could see an expressway. It looked like a lot of farm land. When the pilot said, we were flying over McAllen, Texas, Rell gritted his teeth. He mumbled, "Fuck McAllen."

McAllen looked like it was the only big city in the Valley. There were only three tall buildings downtown, one was all black. We landed and got a rental car. We took 10th street, which was the main road in McAllen, to find some food. We was hungry as hell. We passed by a Plaza Mall, and saw a restaurant off the intersection of 10th and Jackson. Las Casa Del Taco, a Mexican restaurant. We went inside and saw pictures on the wall of some Presidents. Bush, Reagan, Clinton, they'd all eaten here before. The food had to be good. We sat at the bar and looked at the menu. I ordered a Botana Platter, and we waited till I got word where to go. We ate, then got all the directions. They wanted us to go south on 10th street, to take highway 83 west.

We drove until we were in Mission, Texas. We exited on Shary Road. I could see the large houses from a distance. We turned into the Cimarron Country Club, and pulled up to El Chapo's estate.

I had already informed El Chapo that Rell would be coming. He knew who he was and had okayed it. This community was really exclusive. It housed most of the Mexican celebrities, doctors, lawyers, and drug lords.

Getting out of the ride, I felt that jolt of nervousness again.

Rell noticed me jump. "You a'ight, nigga?"

"Yeah, I'm straight, this mafucka crazy, he make me a little nervous," I said.

"Well chill, cause you making me nervous," he said.

I couldn't help but to laugh at him for saying that. We entered the mansion, and it was nothing like the house in Mexico. It was more modern and stylish. I let Rell know to follow my lead, don't get out of pocket down here; it could get us both killed.

The guard escorted us into a sunroom where El Chapo sat waiting with his cigar and tequila.

"Ty, my friend, how are you?" he said when I entered the room.

"I'm cool," I said taking a seat. I pointed to Rell, "This my right hand," I said to El Chapo. He knew Rell already. They had followed us and learned everything about me from that shit with T-Mac.

"Yes, Rell right?" he said.

Rell reached over and shook his hand, then took a seat. I could tell El Chapo was on the edge, he was ordering around his guards more than he usually would.

"Who can you trust these days?" he said.

I shrugged my shoulders.

"Of course, you and Rell don't have that problem with each other right?" he continued. "You take a poor man and make him wealthy, and what does he do? How does he repay you? By stealing money and switching your product." He took a hit of his cigar. "I'm so appreciative that you were there to point that out at the manufacturing area, because I wouldn't have found out that Chavez was a rat." He got up from his seat. "I hear the Cartels have waged a war against me, when they don't have the power," he said, clutching his fist. He waved to us. "You know why I'm against this peace?" he asked.

I didn't answer. I knew he was explaining and talking. Everything had a meaning with this man, and it was no need for me to throw two cents on anything.

"Because everything you do will now have to be discussed between the others. I answer to no man," he yelled. Hatred was brewing in him. He slammed his hands on the table, looking back and forth at me and Rell. "We will meet at a distribution center shortly with the Cartel leaders. I promised them safety, that this will not be a set up." He walked back to the window. "I lied. My nephew will be there, and you, Señor Ty, will now have a chance to take care of him like you should have already," he said, turning around and facing me.

I didn't have a choice now. I didn't have a plan either. I didn't even know what Felix or Meno was up to. All I knew was if I didn't kill Felix, then El Chapo would have my head.

El Chapo left out the room. I leaned over to Rell. "Nigga, this shit gon' pop off, andwhen it does, we gotta bust our way out," I said.

Rell nodded his head.

The guards let us into their arsenal to arm ourselves. Rell picked out two small HK automatic guns. We packed extra clips under our shirts and headed out the door. We left the Cimarron

Country Club, traveling more than ten carloads. The President didn't even roll this tough.

When we pulled up to the warehouse a few miles away, the other Cartel leaders were already there. Guards were everywhere, positioned with guns on lookout. I assumed they were with us, because some of them walked up to open the door for El Chapo. The drivers opened the doors for the other Cartel bosses. They got out and proceeded to the building. Felix looked my way and gave me a slight nod, then kept on walking.

Inside Meno and Juarez were ready and waiting. Meno greeted me and nodded his head with a smirk. If that was a sign, I didn't get it. The room had a large executive table with chairs. The leaders were seated. El Chapo at the head, Meno to the right, the Juarez brothers on the side of Meno, the Gulf Cartel on the side of the Juarez's, then Felix, the Tijuana Cartel leader. Felix and El Chapo made no eye contact at all. I could feel the tension.

Me and Rell would steal glances at each other, covering exits and watching others. I didn't know when to react. If El Chapo wanted me to body Felix, then that's what I would have to do. I couldn't afford to go against the odds, he had the ups on everybody.

The Gulf Cartel and the Juarez Cartel spoke first. One of the Juarez brothers stood up. "El Chapo it's an honor," he said. He took his seat again. "Some of us have risen from nothing to what we are now, and some of us were born into this," he glanced at Felix, who was smiling at the statement. "I have no problem with any of you. We have each built empires that no one but our own can make crumble. And with this war, we are doing just that," he said looking around. "The government has given up any means of a treaty between us and them. So now it's left up to us, to bring this to an end." He leaned back into his seat.

One of the Gulf Cartel leaders, nodded and started to speak. "I agree. We are creating enemies on top of enemies. Families of slain policemen and politicians have come against us. Even the churches have leaked information on us. Soon, we will have no political resources."

Everyone looked on, waiting on Felix or El Chapo to speak. Neither wanted to say anything; they were beyond talking. A brief silence passed, then Felix gave in and started to speak.

"I apologize that it has come to this meeting. Surely I'm young, but I'm experienced as well. So much time has been wasted fighting the government, that millions, maybe billions, has been lost in the process." Felix looked like a feeling of hatred hit him all of a sudden. He looked like El Chapo had at the house, like a burst of rage came over him. "We can not afford to let this arrogance overcome us!"

El Chapo raised up from his seat. He looked fierce. "You insult me with arrogance, coming in here, being in my presence alone. The government is against everything we have built! There will be no treaty!" He looked around at the other leaders, spitting as he continued. "You show weakness! You show fear! When you should show strength and power! No remorse! If they turn against you, so what. Make them fear you more, we will kill all of their families!" El Chapo yelled at all of them.

The leaders had a look of hatred mixed with fear on their faces. They knew they were outnumbered. Felix jumped out of his seat. "You arrogant fool! You would bring more trouble to this already!" He looked at Meno.

Meno glanced at Juarez, and nodded his head.

Rell was about to step up and open fire, but I grabbed him by the arm.

"Fuck this shit, nigga," he whispered.

I gave him a firm look. He knew I was serious. This was not the moment. I could see something else was about to happen.

Juarez stepped over to the door and opened it.

Felix continued to talk. "We have put up with your actions for too long, now your time has run out!"

El Chapo looked at his guards. He pointed to them to grab Felix.

They didn't move.

"You threaten me?" El Chapo yelled at Felix. He looked to his guards again, as they reached for their arms. The other armed men came in the room with guns already drawn on El Chapo and his men. El Chapo looked surprised at his very own men pulling guns on each other.

"What the fuck are you doing?" he yelled. "Get that fucking gun out of my face!"

Meno stepped up.

"Meno, take care of these fucking idiots," El Chapo yelled. Meno turned around and looked at me.

I knew now that was my cue.

Felix smiled.

"You wanted him to kill me, well, the tables have turned," Felix said, cocking his head to me and nodding at El Chapo. "El Moreno."

I walked up to El Chapo and fired a shot into his head. The other Cartel leaders looked at me, surprised.

One of El Chapo's men pulled his gun and shot one of the armed men holding the gun on him.

Rell opened fire on him and the other guards.

Everyone ducked for cover under the table. As the gun exchange went on for a second or two, then it stopped.

The other leaders rose up slowly from cover, looking around. They got up, then walked over the bodies and out of the room. They all shook my hand like I did something they couldn't do. Rell walked out of the room behind me. They were already discussing the treaty. The guards inside were helping to dispose the bodies. Felix approached me and Rell.

"You have showed an excellent amount of loyalty to us, and for that, we are grateful. If it's anything you ever want, just ask."

The other Cartel nodded also.

"Our friend in Baltimore," Felix added, "has some very powerful men asking about him. He is not one of us, so it's best we leave him alone and let them deal with him."

"What are you talking about, very powerful men, the feds?" I asked.

"No, he has been disloyal to Arteaga, an important person and very deadly when disrespected. He is not one of us." Felix said.

I was beginning to like the homie Skills, and I definitely didn't want to leave him dry like this. I felt I had to at least tell him what was up. That wouldn't leave me in any trouble at all.

I glanced around the room at the other Cartel bosses. All of them were huddled around Meno, greeting him and discussing business. Meno looked at me and smiled. He was now the new leader of the Sinaloa Cartel.

Chapter Twenty-One

"Damn," Boo yelled trying to get in the Yukon. He was leaving the hospital in St. Louis. "Nigga, why you come in this big-ass truck? I gotta climb up in this mafucka."

"Nigga, you ain't get nothing but grazed," Chad said.

"Yeah, it don't feel like it though," Boo said. Boo drove himself across the water to a hospital, so he wouldn't get harassed by the cops about the shooting. He knew if he would have went on the East Side, he would probably be fighting a case soon.

"Why them niggas was at you like that?" Chad asked. Chad wanted to suit up and ride on whoever was out in the hood. He was pissed.

"Shit, I don't know, probably was trying to rob a nigga," Boo said. He wanted to change clothes quick. "Take me over to my spot."

"A'ight, first we gotta do this shit for Rell real quick. Gotta meet some bitch named Kimberly."

* * *

Kimberly sat in the Suburban waiting on her contact to call. Rell had said he would be gone and would have his people get in contact with her. She couldn't believe she was being set up to do this. The detective threatened to put her in federal prison for five years if she didn't co-operate. He promised her all she would have to do is wear a wire and conduct business as normal, but try to get names. After a while of sitting in the interrogation room, she'd given in. She knew too many people in prison and heard about the rough time. She wasn't trying to go. The detective wired her phone before she went to pick up the Suburban. Then had her stop back by the station to have the truck wired for sound. Then she left, and now she was waiting on the contact so she could finish what she got herself into. Her phone rang, it was Rell's people telling her where to meet them. She cranked up the Suburban and headed their way.

* * *

"What the fuck Smiley keep rolling by grinning fo?" Tra said, walking back inside the house.

Geezy was coming from out the kitchen. "Man, where the fuck is the nigga Kill at wit my food?" he asked. "I'm hungry as fuck."

"He sho' been gone for a minute. Hit that nigga and see what's up," Tra said.

* * *

"Let me get a twenty piece, with all the sides," Kill said to the lady at the counter. He kept looking back at the two Centralia niggas sitting and eating. One of them had pointed to him when he came through the door. He wasn't tripping off them two. He could punish two Centralia cats. He answered his phone.

"What up, nigga?" he said. Geezy was on the line, trying to see how long he was gon' be with the food. "I'm on my way, fam, these Centralia niggas up in here staring at a nigga and shit." He didn't look around, or he would have noticed the car load of dudes coming inside. They stormed right over to him and snuck him with a hook to the jaw. He dropped the phone, stumbling into the counter. "Punk-ass nigga," he yelled, throwing some blows back at the guy who hit him. He hit him with a combination, until the others stepped in and jumped on him. They was kicking and stumping him.

Geezy and Tra pulled up on the lot. When Kill dropped the phone Geezy knew he was getting his ass whooped.

The Centralia niggas saw them getting out the ride and tried to run out the door. Geezy caught one of them coming out with a hook, knocking him off his feet. Tra chased down one of the dudes, clipping him from behind, then he started to beat his ass. Kill got up and came out to join in.

They heard the sirens coming, and everyone took off, except the ones that were either wounded or knocked out. Tra and Kill were in their rides when Tra pulled up on the side of Kill.

"Where the fuck Geezy at?" Kill yelled.

Kill looked up and saw Geezy running out the door with the twenty piece Kill had ordered.

"Nigga fuck that food," Kill yelled.

"Man, come on," Tra said.

Geezy got inside.

"Shit, nigga, fuck y'all. I'm hungry as fuck," Geezy said.

* * *

Chad loaded up the Suburban while Boo counted the money to make sure it was all there. Kimberly sat nervously, trying to maintain her composure. She had everything the detective wanted on the wire. Them counting the money and stating how much they were giving her, and them saying their names. Chad had been smacking her on the ass and trying to holla at her. She would move his hand and tell him Rell would get mad.

Chad just replied, "That's my nigga, he ain't gone give a fuck." Chad approached her again. "I'm saying when you get back, why don't you stop over?" He grabbed her ass again.

"Boy, please, what Rell gone say?" she said. She was hoping he didn't get real fresh with her. She didn't want him to see she was nervous and suspect something. She kept her phone in her hand the whole time.

"Like I said, he ain't tripping," Chad said. He reached for her phone. "Here, let me put my number in yo' phone, so you can call my other number whenever you want."

She snatched it away quickly and started to stutter her words. "I'll put it in there myself, what is it?"

He gave her the number.

"I'll call you when I get back, straight up," she said, grabbing her things. "Can I get paid?" She wasn't supposed to get the money until she got back from the delivery. She wanted to see if they knew that.

Boo yelled out, "Hell naw, when you get back." He didn't want Chad to give in to that bitch. Boo was thinking she was going to run off.

Kimberly tried her hand, it didn't work. She wanted the money now, so that she could take care of the last drop, turn in the wire, then disappear.

* * *

"Yo, where the fuck is Story at?" Skills asked one of the young workers on his block. He pulled up to see if everything been going okay since he'd been gone. He was in the Park Heights area. The little shorty ran up to the truck.

"I don't know, I ain't seen him in a couple of days. We had to holla at Jason for our re-up."

"What? Holla at Jason, a'ight, you straight out here?" Skills asked, wondering if they still had enough dope to work. Story was in charge of dropping off the packs to the shorties. Jason kept an eye on the safe house in the hood. They were never supposed to go holla at Jason for anything, that would make the safe house noticeable.

The little nigga shook his head. "Yeah we straight."

Skills wondered what the fuck been going on while he been gone. He knew that Story had been acting strange ever since he landed the connect with Shai.

"You be cool, and watch out for them jakes," Skills said to the shorty, then pulled off.

He picked up the box with the watches inside. He didn't know how to approach Shai at all. She was too unpredictable. He knew where they stayed, from the last time they'd met, and she didn't go too far from her house. When he pulled off, he just happened to take the direction to her home and peeped her truck in the driveway. He decided to ride by and get the address, so that he could mail them to her. He boxed them up and gift wrapped them. After that, he went to a florist and ordered a dozen mixed roses and had them delivered along with the watches.

"What would you like on the card, sir?" the florist asked.

Skills was stuck. He didn't want to say some corny shit. He didn't think Shai would fall for that slick talking shit either. She seemed like a different type of chick. He took the card and wrote:

"Let's start all over, meet me at ten tonight, at the Harbor."

Shai and Moni sat watching television. When the doorbell rang, Moni jumped. They were watching a horror flick.

"Girl, yo' scary ass, scared me," Shai said, as she got up and peeped out the side window by the door. The florist delivery guy stood there with the roses and a box in his hands. Shai ran to the couch. She lifted the pillow up and grabbed the .45 caliber Smith & Wesson. Moni jumped up this time, and she hurried to the door, too. She knew what time it was.

Shai hid behind the door, then nodded at Moni when she was ready for her to open it. A florist delivery. Shai didn't trust that at all.

Moni opened the door. "Hello, may I help you?" her hand sat on the back of the door.

Shai looked at them waiting for the tap.

"Hi, is Shai's home?" he said.

"Yes! I'm Shai," Moni lied.

"These are for you, as well as this," he said, handing her the roses and the box. Moni cuffed them in her hand, then signed for the gifts.

"Thank you, who are they from?" Moni asked, trying to find out who knew the address.

"Uh," the florist said, looking at the clipboard, "I don't know exactly, I wasn't at work when they were ordered, I'm just the delivery guy." He smiled and walked off.

Moni closed the door.

"Girl, somebody know where we at," Moni said. She wasn't shocked at all. Kristy had a big mouth, and since that shit happened with her and Shai, she really probably was loose at the lips. They had already been looking for a new house, but nothing came up yet. Moni looked at the card. "Let's start all over, meet me at ten tonight, at the Harbor," Moni read aloud.

Shai put the pistol back under the pillow. She grabbed the box and sat it down on the table. She read the note. Moni reached for the box.

"Uh, that ain't for you," Shai said smiling.

"Girl, please," Moni said, picking the box up.

As Shai studied the note, she thought about Skills. That's the only nigga who could do some shit like this. "If that nigga followed me home," she thought, "I'mma snap on his ass." No one was supposed to know. Kristy, she thought about Kristy. She couldn't be mad at Skills if he got it from Kristy's hoe ass. Moni ripped the wrapping from the box. At the sight of the emblem encrusted on the suede box, she gasped. She opened it slowly. When she saw the watches, she almost dropped the box.

"Shai, girl, look at this," Moni said.

Shai held the flowers and the note, still trying to figure if Skills followed her or not. She turned around. "What is it? Some cheap-ass—" She dropped the roses and the note when she saw the twin diamond Piaget watches that she had received from Ty on her birthday.

* * *

Story watched as Lil Jus made the sell. He whistled to another dude standing by, and the guy ran Story's direction to get the stash. He ran around the building right into Story.

"What the fuck, yo, "he said, trying to make out Story's face. "What the fuck you doing nigga?" the dude asked Story.

"You know what it is," Story said, lifting the burna at him. "Skills wants his spot back bitch." He popped the dude twice, then ran out into the street after he pulled his Scully down, and gunned down Lil Jus on the sidewalk. He snatched the money out of his pockets and ran off. He knew others would say it was a robbery, and he knew they would come at Skills, first.

Chapter Twenty-Two

Shai stared at the watches. She remembered everything about the night she'd received them. She remembered what she wore, what Ty wore, the gifts, the cars, the argument. She ran her fingers along the bezels. She started to get teary-eyed. All the memories came back. Then it hit her. This could be Ty, who else could it be? These watches were one of a kind. There was no other pair in the world like them. She got up and ran upstairs to change.

"What's wrong?" Moni asked, startled at how she hopped up.

Shai stopped at the steps. "Girl, what if Ty is still alive?"

* * *

"Yo, Skills been looking for you, where you been?" one of the lookouts for the safe house said.

Story walked up on the stoop.

"Yeah, where he at?" Story asked.

"I don't know. He said for me to tell you to hit him when I see you," he said.

"Yeah, hey, you straight?" Story asked. He looked up at the door. "Who's in the house?"

"Jason, why what's up?" he said.

"Come on, I gotta holla at you," Story said, walking inside the house. The shorty followed him in. Jason got up from the couch when Story came in with the lookout.

"Why you ain't at ya post, lil man?" Jason asked the shorty.

"Story," the lil shorty said.

Story walked over to the cabinets. He found the dope inside. "You know, somebody just got at them Druid Hill niggas, yo," Story said.

Jason looked up. If somebody just got at them cats, there was gon' be repercussions. Whoever they thought did it, it would be on for real. "You know who?" Jason asked.

"Yeah," Story said, pulling out his Sig Sauer .357. Jason didn't see it until the flame hopped out the barrel. The shorty looked on in shock, then he turned around and tried to run. Story shot him in the back. He walked in the kitchen and grabbed the dope out of the cabinets. He packed it away and left. He knew by tonight it was going down. He had to find out where Skills was, so he could let them niggas from Druid Hill know.

Story figured Skills was still chasing that bitch Shai. He decided it was time to get his revenge on the bitch.

* * *

I tried Skills's phone several times. I had forgotten we found the phone in the couch that day we got set up by Melanie. Now I would have to wait till he called me, with a new number. I wanted to warn him about that dude Arteaga. I wasn't supposed to intervene, but I'd fucked with Skills, and he was an alright dude. He was cool to be around. He hustled hard and came with that money on time, and he seemed like a loyal nigga. I had to help him out, I just had to do it on my own.

* * *

Kimberly got back in her Mazda, and Freaky G ran out of the house, waving at her. She was about to pull out fast, thinking that they found out. She was getting real paranoid.

"Hey, tell them niggas we need to holla," he said.

She pulled out the driveway relieved. She hit the corner on her way to the station. The detectives swarmed her before she made it there. He opened the door to her car.

"Step out for me, Ms. Barker," he said.

She got out.

The detectives were putting on gloves and had a drug dog on the scene.

"What-what's going on? I got what you wanted," she said nervously. One of the men came over and placed cuffs on her.

"Ms. Barker, you're under arrest," he said.

He was dressed in plain clothes, but she tried to take a closer look at his badge. She looked around to observe the others. Smiley shook his head and grabbed her phone.

"Here it is," he said, handing it to the officer that cuffed her. Smiley looked at Kimberly. "I did what I could, your co-operation will still help you out," Smiley said. "The D.E.A. wanted the case, it's over my head."

"What! Wha! You motherfucker! You set me up from the gate," she jerked in her cuffs, "What's that supposed to mean, over your head?"

Affiliated II

The D.E.A. agent grabbed her putting her in the car. "That means thanks, but you're still going to prison."

* * *

Kristy answered the door. She had been laying low ever since that ass-whooping from Shai. Her crew had criticized her about the scars, and what they would have done if it were them. She was tired of hearing that shit. She opened the door. It was Story. She fucked with Story now. He was the only person who came through and checked on her from time to time, even though he would always want some head or pussy. She didn't mind; she wanted the dick.

"Hey, what you up to?" she asked, opening the door for him to come in.

"Shit! Just checking on you and coming to holla at you about something," Story said.

"About what?" Kristy asked, while walking back to the kitchen. She was cooking some food.

"You know some niggas out to get Skills right?" he said.

"Uh-uh, who?" she said, coming from around the counter like this was the news of the day.

"I don't know, but I do know they think that Moni his gal, and they plotting on getting her," Story said. He'd found out the other day that her and Moni still talked. He figured she would want to warn Moni, so she wouldn't get hurt. She didn't like Shai, but she wouldn't let nothing really bad happen to family.

"What? I gotta call her and tell her," she said, looking for her phone.

"Naw! It's best we go check on her for real. This shit is supposed to go down tonight. Try to call her first, but you best go over there," he said.

She threw the phone down. "You right," she said, leaving the room to go and put some clothes on.

Story just sat there smiling. Soon, he would take over Skills's spots. He would to get his revenge on the bitch Shai first, then lock in the connect with Arteaga.

* * *

Kristy pulled up to Moni's. She got out and hurried to the door and started knocking repeatedly.

Moni looked out the window beside the door. She paused when she saw who it was.

Kristy yelled through the door. "Open the door, please, I need to talk to you, Moni!"

Moni opened the door. "What? I thought I told you don't come over here no more."

"I know! I know! But it's important, I need to talk to you. You might be in trouble, can I come in?" she asked. Moni paused for a minute to think about letting her inside. She looked out the door and over to her car. Nobody was with her, so she stepped to the side to let her in.

"Hurry up," Moni said. She let Kristy pass by her and turned around to watch her every move. She no longer trusted Kristy. Moni faced her while closing the door. Neither one expected it when Story to hopped out of nowhere.

He pushed in on the door with his gun in the air.

"Story, what the fuck you doing?" Kristy yelled. "What you doing here?"

"Shut the fuck up, bitch," he said, pointing the gun at Moni's head. "Where that bitch Shai at?"

Moni just looked at Kristy. She couldn't believe that her own blood would set her up.

Story pressed the barrel to her head harder. "Where she at?" he asked again.

"Story, what the fuck is going on?" Kristy yelled.

"Bitch I said," Story reached over and hit her in the mouth with the gun, "Shut up!"

Moni saw that as an opportunity to run for her gun. She took off, but Story was tall and agile. He caught her right before she was about to grab it. "Come here, bitch!" He grabbed her by the neck, forcing her down to the floor. "What the fuck was you going for, huh?" he said. He turned over a pillow on the couch and found Moni's gun. "Yeah," he said as he kicked Moni in the side.

"I got something for you," he said, pulling her by her hair. Moni glanced over at Kristy, she was lying semi-conscious, barely moving. Story forced Moni to sit in the dining chair. He tore a piece of cloth and tied her hands down. He then pulled out a syringe and some dope and sat it on the table. He went over and grabbed Kristy by the throat.

She started to gag for air.

He dragged her to another chair and tied her up. "Let me show you how we do it in the B-More," he said to Moni. He prepared a needle, thumping it several times, then squirting a little out. "Yeah, it's that shit," he said, pulling up Kristy's sleeve. He stuck Kristy in the arm with the syringe and pressed all the dope into her.

Kristy screamed.

"I ain't gotta tell you shut up this time," he said. "This shit shit will in a minute."

Kristy's eyes rolled back into her head. Her head started to twirl around. It was too much to handle uncut. Some of the best couldn't take this batch. Kristy gasped for air.

Tears started to leak down Moni's face as she watched her lil cousin suffer a slow death by overdose.

Kristy gasped. Her body jolted like she got hit with electricity, then she went limp.

Moni balled up her fist, trying to pull herself from the ties.

Story looked at Moni. "Now. You gon' tell me where ya girl at," he said. He tapped another needle, then sat it back down.

"Fuck you," Moni hissed. She spit at him.

Story grabbed her throat.

"Dumb bitch, I got something for you!" he said, grabbing the other needle. He pulled out another pack. "Yeah, this shit right here. Ain't that how y'all say it, right here," he giggled. "Country-ass mafuckas. You mafuckas from St. Louis fucking up my shit. It's cool, though, you don't deserve a fast death. I'mma give you that slow shit!" He laughed. "That fifteen to twenty year shit." He prepared the dope.

Moni looked at the needle. It looked like it had dried blood on it.

"Yeah, this shit wouldn't be going on if ya girl wouldn't have set my man up with that nigga in St. Louis," Story said. "Nigga fucking up my shit."

She took it all in, what he just said, "that nigga in St. Louis." Shai didn't know who Meno had hooked Skills up with. Moni thought was it possible.

Story smacked Moni.

"Hey, bitch, before I let yo' ass go to waste, I'mma give you a little present," he said, pulling out his dick. He ripped her clothes off, then tied both her legs up to the chair.

Moni sat there with her legs wide open.

"Before I hit you with this needle, that's infected with that monster, that full blown. I'mma see what I'm about to throw away." He rammed her hard until he came.

Moni bit her lip until it bled. She didn't want to show any sign or reaction. She only wanted to show anger. Her eyes were fire red, and her face was soaked from the tears. When Story finished, he let loose inside of her. He grabbed the needle and smiled after he pulled up his pants.

"Tell my son, if you don't have a miscarriage first, that his daddy was a mafucka," he said as he pulled out the syringe, loading the dope into the needle. "Don't trip, baby momma, you gon' love it and need it." He laughed as he tapped the needle.

Moni started to jerk in the chair, trying to get free.

"No motherfucka," she yelled.

–BANG—the needle fell out of Story fingers.

–BANG—BANG—

Moni tried to turn around to see who, but couldn't. Story's eyes bulged out of his face at the sight of Shai holding a gun with the barrel smoking. He stumbled into the china cabinet, then fell to the floor.

Moni started to jerk in her chair again. Shai came around and untied Moni. Moni snatched the gun and fired several more shots into Story body. He jerked until the last shot.

"Girl. He ain't hit you wit that shit, did he?" Shai asked, looking at Kristy.

"Naw! He was about to, though, God Shai!" Moni started to cry. She hugged Shai tightly.

"Oh," she sighed as she looked at Kristy.

Shai wondered what was going on.

Chapter Twenty-Three

"Hurry up, Boo," Chad yelled. They were on their way to the airport to pick up Rell and Ty. Boo came out limping.

"Nigga they ain't even call yet, what you rushing for?" Boo said, getting in the ride.

"Yeah, they said they'll be landing in a couple of hours, and it's been a hour already," Chad said, pulling off.

"What the fuck," Chad said, seeing a unmarked fly past in front of him. He hit reverse and punched it to see another one in the back. He whipped the wheel, turning into a yard and going around the unmarked car, then slammed the gas.

"What the fuck, that's D.E.A.," Boo yelled, looking back at the officer trying to get out of his car. Chad looked back at the unmarked car.

"Watch out," Boo yelled as another car blocked them off. He was too late, and the truck smacked into the side of the Explorer.

All the agents hopped out, surrounding the car with their guns drawn. "Get out of the vehicle now, with ya hands up, put ya hands up!" an agent yelled, opening the door to the truck.

Chad and Boo got out with their hands in the air. Chad was held by the back of his shirt as the agent walked him to the front of the truck. Soon as the agent took his hands off his shirt, Chad took off.

"We got a runner," the agent yelled.

Several took off, chasing Chad with their tasers in hand. One of the agents looked at Boo with the taser on him. "You want to run!?" he asked.

Boo knew he couldn't run anyway, and he looked at the agent, then at the gun. The agent probably had the voltage turned all the way up. "Hell naw," Boo said.

Shortly after the run, they brought Chad back. He looked like they'd tased him repeatedly. They placed them in the back seat of one of the cars and started to applaud each other on a good job.

"Mafuckas," Chad mumbled, lying his head back into the seat.

* * *

"Turn that shit down, nigga," Tra yelled at Kill.

Kill turned the music up louder, reciting the lyrics. "This nigga insane, yeah, a straight fool-half a million dollar car, in some house shoes."

Geezy joined in on reciting the lyrics. They broke down everything and packed it up.

"Man, let's get that shit out of here," Geezy said.

"Man, fuck dat. We rolling tonight," Tra said. He started to join in on the lyrics. "This nigga insane, yeah a straight fool." He rapped as he walked back in the other room.

Geezy walked in the kitchen to get something to drink. When he opened the refrigerator, he heard someone yelling.

"Police! Get down now," the cops coming through the door yelled.

Tra heard the cops. He ran to the bathroom and tried to flush the drugs down the toilet, but Smiley opened the bathroom door and tackled him into the tub.

Geezy tried to run out the back door and found himself surrounded by agents.

"Get the fuck down, now," one of the agents yelled.

The agents walked them outside one by one, escorting them into the patrol cars. The whole neighborhood watched on as they raided the house. After a while of searching the residence, they came out with more drugs and paraphernalia. They patted each other on the back as the others came down the steps with drugs. Smiley knocked on the back windows of the patrol cars that Geezy, Kill, and Tra was sitting in.

He just smiled at them and waved.

* * *

I'd been calling Boos and Chad's phones for about an hour.

Rell called the spots, but nobody answered there either. "What the fuck these niggas doing?" Rell asked, stepping out of the baggage claim.

"Let me try 'em again," I said.

Rell flagged down a cab.

"Come on, nigga," he yelled.

I hung up the phone and grabbed my bag. We got home, and I dropped the bag at the door.

Rell tried calling their phones again while I went in the kitchen to fix me a drink.

"What's up?" I asked taking a seat when I came back.

"I don't know. They still ain't answered," Rell said. "Oh, let me check and see if they got up with the bitch Kimberly." He called her phone, he got no answer.

* * *

D.E.A. agent Boone sat at the desk observing the cellphones from the bust. In the last hour, the same number had called three of the phones on the desk. He got up to tell his boss. They came back in the office, and he pulled the cell phones to the side and picked up each one individually. "This number called back to back on all of these phones," he said, showing his boss the phones.

"Who's phones are they?" his boss asked.

"These phones came from Chad and Boo, and this one is off our girl," he said.

"Who do you think it is?" his boss asked.

"I think it's the head guy we're looking for, the one in charge."

His boss nodded his head with his hand on his chin.

"Yeah, me too," he said. "Look, get her up here a.s.a.p. and see if she can get him on a call," the boss said.

Agent Boone hurried out of the office. He got on the elevator and went down to the holding cells.

"I'm bout to pull out Ms. Barker," he said to the guard.

"Alright," the guard said, getting up and walking towards the holding area. He hit a button and the large metal door slid back. "Ms. Barker, Ms. Barker, come on, come with me," the guard said.

Kimberly got up from the mat. She'd been asleep, dreaming of being at home. She stood up, wiped her mouth, and looked around at the walls. Her face had a print of the mat on the side. She stepped out the cell, and the guard pointed to the door. She turned and walked out. She saw agent Boone, and instant hatred filled her. He was the officer who had arrested her.

"Ms. Barker can you come with me for a minute?" he said.

"You act like I got a choice," she replied sarcastically.

He tried to laugh. "I guess not, but I'm being polite," he said. They got on the elevator, he pressed the button. "Sleeping good?" he asked.

"Yeah," Kimberly said, sarcastically again.

"I'm sorry to wake you, it's just something we gotta talk about. Do you have any kids?" he asked.

"Nope," she said.

"Was one of them your boyfriend or something?" he asked.

"Nope." She rolled her eyes at him.

"I'm sorry, I was just curious as to why you risked your life and freedom to do that. You should've been in college or something, working on a family and enjoying life," he said.

Kimberly didn't say anything.

"I'm just trying to help you out," he added.

"Well, let me go," she said.

"That's up to you," he said as the elevator door opened. "Right this way." He pointed towards the office. She came in and saw her cellphone on the desk.

"Have a seat," his boss said to her.

She looked back as another agent entered the room.

"Look, you can help us and help yourself, or you can go to prison for these guys. But I'm telling you, they're not going to go to jail for you." He watched to see if she was buying it. "Someone called your phone several times," he said as he picked up the phone and showed it to her. "You recognize the number?" he asked.

Kimberly looked at it. She knew it well. It was Rell. she loved Rell and didn't want to hurt him, but she didn't want to go to prison either.

"No, I don't," she said.

"Come on, this person called your phone—" she cut him off.

"I said I don't know. Why the fuck you got me here, you bout to let me go?"

"That depends, do you know the number?" he asked.

"Is you gon' let me go?" she asked again, moving her head to the side.

"Look, if you help us we can help you," he said.

"Help me get out?" she asked.

The boss nodded his head and shrugged his shoulders. "Yeah, we would do our best to help you get out," he said. "All you need to do is call this number and get him to talk about the drop." Kimberly thought about it. She could go home, free. Home. She looked at the phone.

"Okay," she whispered.

"What?" he asked. "I didn't hear,"

"I said okay!"

The other guy hooked a plug into the bottom of the phone, then pressed a button on the phone. He held up one finger, then gave her the phone.

"If he asks why you haven't answered the phone, just tell 'em you were sleeping," he said.

She looked at them and smirked. She picked up the phone, staring at the number, then pressed send.

* * *

Rell's phone finally started to buzz.

"This that bitch Kimberly right here," he said. He answered the phone. "What's up?"

"Hey, you called?" she asked.

"Yeah, what's going on?" he asked.

"Nothing, just was sleep, I did that already," she said. She waved her hand at the agent that was trying to tell her to speed up the conversation.

"Did what? Where you at? I'mma come holla at you," he said.

She paused and looked at the agents. One rolled his hand at her, trying to tell her to keep going. Inside, Kimberly knew they wouldn't let her go. Her hatred grew. "Thanks," Agent Boone had said, "but you're still going to prison." She looked around at the agents in the room. They sat patiently, anticipating her response. She took a deep breath.

"I can't come meet you right now, the D.E.A. here," she said, then hung up.

The agents lowered their heads. Agent Boone got up from the desk and walked around to Kimberly. He pulled her out of the chair, reached to his side, and got his cuffs, slapping them on her wrist.

"I hope you think about what you just did every day in prison," he said.

Kimberly looked around at all of the agents. "Fuck all y'all," she said.

* * *

Rell hung up the phone. He couldn't believe what he'd just heard her say. The D.E.A. Shit. He looked at me.

"Damn, Chad'n'em might be jammed up. Kimberly with the D.E.A."

"What?" I said.

"Yeah, she just said the D.E.A. with her," he pulled out the battery in his phone, I did the same to mine. We stomped the phones and broke the SIM cards. We didn't know what had been said already. Kimberly couldn't know much, besides the shit in Mt. Vernon. I knew Rell wouldn't let that bitch in on too much; he knew better.

We got up and got all the change together, just in case they knew too much already. We loaded and moved everything to different spots. We stashed all the money we had hidden around in a safe spot.

Rell wanted to swing by his spot out in Westport. He had a tri-level condominium out there. I saw all the lights and sirens at his spot from the highway before we got there.

"Damn," Rell said, hitting the dash. "That bitch Kimberly."

"What, you brought that bitch to yo spot?" I asked.

"Yeah, after the club one night, I had her meet me out at the crib. But she ain't know how to get out here. She used the GPS on her phone to do the directions. I ain't know this bitch was gon' be handling business for a nigga." He leaned back into the seat.

I got off and turned to get back on the highway to get another peek.

"You think she telling?" I asked.

"I don't know. The bitch warned me, and now this shit throwing me off,"he said.

"Well, somebody ratted you out," I said. "Let's get up with the lawyer and find out if it's anything that popped up with you or me."

I know my nigga didn't have anything at the crib. He was more careful than I was. I didn't know what the others told the D.E.A., though. We talked about the possibility of Chad and Boo, but we felt they were solid. They never would rat.

Geezy'n'em didn't know shit about us at all, so we wasn't worried. Kimberly was the only one who could link Rell with the charges. If she kept quiet, we'd be cool. We had Chad's and Boo's names run through the computer. It showed they had cases pending. Conspiracy with the intent to distribute and drug trafficking an excess of five kilograms of cocaine and five kilograms of heroin. The lawyer gave us every name on the case and Kimberly's name, Kimberly Barker. He warned us to beware if she knew anything. There was a possibility that we could be brought up on these same charges.

I paced the office, thinking about Chad and Boo. I had to get them out of this situation. I could use my connections with the Cartels to help them out, but then again, that could get them killed. The Cartels only helped those who were important to them and their business. They didn't know Chad and Boo, cousins of Shai or not, they didn't matter to the Cartels. They could easily see them as a liability, thinking they would leak information on me, which in turn would put them in another predicament. After that, I probably wouldn't be a factor either. If it was just up to Meno, I would try to plead for them, but the treaty meant it was up to all of them.

It was best for me to stay out of the way and make sure they were okay.

"I want you to check up on them and get the best lawyer possible," I said."I don't care what it costs, or where he's from. I want you to find out a way to beat this case for them."

Chapter Twenty-Four

Skills sat at home, waiting to hear from one of his workers on Story. He searched all over for Story, but he couldn't find him. After Shai didn't show up last night, he figured she wasn't interested at all. It was time to just let her be and fuck with the connect, business as usual. He'd heard them Druid Hill niggas was at him. He didn't want to believe Story had something to do with that, but after hearing it was Story that hit his safe house, he figured Story was the one trying to blame the Druid Hill robbery on him. Shawn, the little nigga that was on lookout for the safe house had survived the shot in the back. He was the one who'd informed Skills of Story being the one who hit the house.

He heard a knock on the door. He got up, lifting the beretta to his side. He crept to the door and stood to the side of the doorway. He peeped out. When he saw who it was, he opened the door quickly.

"What you doing here?" he asked.

Shai stood in the doorway, staring past him into the apartment.

"Come in," Skills said, opening the door wide.

"I would've met you last night, but something went down, so I just followed you," Shai said. Shai looked at Skills's gun before she passed through the door into the house.

"Oh, I'm sorry," he said, putting the gun in his back pocket. When he put the gun up, Shai tapped on the doorsill before she entered.

Moni popped out with her gun drawn on Skills.

"Don't move," she said calmly.

"What?" he said.

Shai came in with her gun out, reaching around Skills and pulling his gun out his back pocket. "Shai, what the fuck is you on?" he asked.

"Naw, what the fuck is you on?" she yelled back. "I should let my girl blast yo' punk ass for what happened to her and Kristy. Where did you get these?" Shai asked, holding up the watches.

"For what? Her and Kristy? What the fuck is you talking about?" Skills looked at the watches. She recognized them. He'd known deep down that she and Pablo had some kind of connection.

Shai stepped up to Skills and pressed the gun to the back of his head.

"Where?" she yelled.

BOOM! A loud bang rang through the apartment. Shai, Moni, and Skills ducked for cover, scattering around the room. She looked at the hole in the door; it was the size of a volleyball.

Someone kicked the door in. Three armed gunmen stepped in the room. A big muscular guy held a riot gauge, a shorter guy held two handguns, and the one who stayed out in the hall was a tall, slim, black guy.

Shai was on the other side of the room. Her gun had fallen out of her hand during the shotgun blast. She looked for Moni and saw her lying on the floor against a wall, holding her side and breathing heavy. She still had her gun in her hand. She'd been hit by buckshot during the blast. There was no way Shai could get to Moni or to her gun. She didn't know who these dudes were, or if they were just coming to kill. She saw no sign of Skills. "Scary mafucka," she whispered.

Someone grabbed her hair, pulling her up from the hiding spot.

"Please, please don't kill me, don't kill me,"she screamed, trying to sound like a scared tramp.

"Shut the fuck up," the tall slim dude said, walking through the door. "Where's Skills?" he said it like he'd asked this question already a million times. The big muscular guy held her in the air by her hair.

"I don't know, I swear," Shai said. She looked around and saw her gun lying at her feet. The third guy walked back in.

"He ain't here," he said, looking at Moni. Shai thought to herself how cowardly Skills was. She was sure to kill him whenever she caught up with him.

The tall slim dude looked around. "Alright, dust these bitches off and let's roll," he said.

Shai kicked the big dude right in the nuts. He let go of her, and she dropped for the gun. Moni sat up and dropped two shots in the third dude. The tall one ducked out the door, firing back.

Shai grabbed her gun. The big guy raised the gauge and shot missing Shai by inches. Shai dropped to the floor and unloaded the clip in the big dude. He fell down with a loud thump.

The tall dude came back in.

Moni saw him and tried to shoot, but she was out of bullets.

He had his gun his gun drawn on Shai. He stepped over her. "Motherfucking bitch," he yelled.

–BANG-

* * *

"Get this shit out of my face, "Chad said to the guard, smacking the tray out of his hand.

"Lock down," the guard yelled at Chad.

"Fuck lock down, bitch," Chad yelled. He was pissed. They'd separated him and Boo, being held without a bond, and they had a federal hold on them. The guard left and came back with a few other guards. They had tasers in their hands.

"Lock down, now," he yelled.

Chad looked at them and the tasers, he walked to his room and locked down. He didn't want to feel that taser again.

He had commissary all over the cell. He was getting $200 dollar money orders in every other day that he had to sign for. They had alias names on them, but he knew who they were from. He laid down and hit the top bunk.

"Hey, man," his white celly said, jumping up out of his sleep.

"Shut the fuck up fo' I beat yo ass," Chad said.

* * *

Boo laid in the bunk reading an urban book. His celly had a lot of the street novels for Boo to read. Boo enjoyed reading them; he was doing most of the shit they were writing about. He told his celly that he should write a book.

Boo got up to the sound of his door sliding open and a guard calling his name for a lawyer visit. He got up and put his shirt on and went to see who it was. He hadn't gotten a lawyer yet and hadn't talked to no one but a couple of bitches on the phone.

All he knew was he had money on his books. Every two days, he received a receipt for $200 dollars being placed on his account. He knew it was from Rell and Ty. He would spend it all on commissary and phone cards, so he could call bitches and get them to play with their pussy. He didn't have Ty's or Rell's numbers, and he didn't try to call the old numbers either. He knew to keep them in the clear until he found out what was going on.

The guard nodded to the lawyer. "I'm okay. I got it from here," the lawyer said. He was a short, stocky build and looked to be Jewish or Italian. "Hey, I'm Mr. Roschild, I'm your hired attorney," he said, extending his hand out to Boo.

Boo shook his hand and took a seat.

"I haven't gotten in touch with your brother or cousin, he's in another county, but I will," the lawyer said. "Ask if you need anything." The lawyer leaned into the table, "like cigarettes or anything like that."

Boo nodded, but he didn't respond to that.

"I'm going to do my best to help you two get out of this. Now, to my understanding I'm getting paid to beat this case, but I need to know from you, do you want to fight it?"

"Shit, what I'm facing?" Boo asked.

"Well, you both have the same charges, conspiracy, trafficking with the intent to distribute an excess of five kilograms of cocaine and five kilograms of heroin. You're looking at anywhere, between ten to twenty years, depending on your background."

Boo sat there thinking. "Twenty years, fuck, ten at the least."

"Shit," Boo said, "if you can beat it, hell yeah, let's go!"

* * *

Shai looked at the chest of the tall dude, through a smoking hole in it. Skills stood on the other side, barely staying up with the gauge in his hands. He held his stomach. It must have happened when the first shotgun blast went off, because he'd been standing right by Moni. He fell to the floor and rolled over.

Shai got up and helped Moni to her feet. They tried to help Skills get up.

"Naw," let me go." He coughed.

"We can get you to a hospital," Moni said.

"Naw, fuck it, get out of here 'fore the cops come. Hurry up, I'll be straight," he said.

Shai looked at him; she was speechless. He had saved her life. As bad as she wanted to interrogate him about the watches, she grabbed her gun, found the watches, and she and Moni left out the door.

* * *

Skills knew the Druid Hill niggas would be at him for good now. There was no way around a peace. One of their head dudes lay dead in his apartment. He rolled over. The wound in his stomach was bleeding badly. He stumbled down the stairs and out the door, where he got his keys out and got in the truck. He took a deep breath and let his head fall on the headrest.

"Fuck," he whispered to himself. He started the truck.

Someone was approaching the truck. Mendez, Arteaga's henchman.

He threw the ride in drive, seeing Mendez pulling out a glock and aiming it at him. He ducked down to the side as Mendez started shooting at the truck. Skills pulled off and sped down the street. Mendez kept firing at the truck's back window, hoping to hit him and see the truck crash into a pole. Skills sped on around the corner. Mendez heard the sirens and fell back to the side of the building.

Skills arrived at the hospital and fell into the emergency room doors. The nurses helped him onto a stretcher. After a few hours, he was bandaged and feeling better. He leaned up and looked out the door. He could see a detective sitting and reading a paper, waiting to hear that he was awake. The nurse came in, and Skills played sleep. She checked the I.V.'s and turned around to check his bandages. Skills jumped up and grabbed her arm before she turned around to leave.

"Shh," Skills said, holding his finger up.

The nurse was about to scream.

"I need your help, please," Skills said.

She looked like she was from the hood, possibly someone that knew or heard about him, because she nodded, saying okay.

"I need you to try and get that cop's attention, so I can get out of here," he said.

* * *

"Damn, girl," Moni said. They had to get a hotel room for the time being. Moni was leaning back in the chair while Shai put gauze on her wounds. Luckily, none of the buckshot had penetrated deep. She had nothing but bruises and minor cuts.

"I ain't no doctor, but you should be straight," Shai said.

Moni looked at the I.D.'s they had.

"These I.D.'s burnt up, and we don't have no other aliases, so what we gon' do now?" she asked.

"We don't need one," Shai said, looking at the watches on the dresser.

"I thought we—" Moni was cut off.

"Meno, he lied to us, Moni, something is going on with him and Ty, and Meno don't want us to know about it," Shai said.

* * *

Skills saw the nurse walk out to the detective. He watched as she started to spark a conversation with him. The detective turned towards her as she showed him a chart. While they were talking, the nurse waved her hand at him to go ahead and get out. He got out the bed and grabbed his keys. He crept along the wall and out the room. Skills hopped on the elevator, then got off and made it to the truck.

"Aww, shit," he mumbled, getting into the truck. He didn't know how bad the wounds were. He just knew he had to get out of there. He had to get some help on dealing with Arteaga. If Arteaga wanted him dead, there was no way out of it. He tried calling Pablo, but got no answer. He tried to call T, also and still got no answer. The only other phone he knew was the number to the phone in the Maserati. He'd learned the number when he was fucking with the navigation the day he was going out to the Steak House. He tried it and got no answer.

"Shit," he said, hitting the steering wheel. He knew he was as good as dead out there alone. If Arteaga didn't get him, the cops would.

He headed out to the only other spot he knew about. No one would find him in Dundalk, Maryland. He had an aunt that stayed there. It was a low key spot.

Chapter Twenty-Five

"It's going to be hard to beat this case," Mr. Roschild said to me.

"What you mean, it's gon' be hard?" I asked.

"Well, most of the evidence is on them. They have them on wires, and they have drugs almost in the quantity they mentioned in the tape," he said.

"What they looking at?" I asked.

"Ten, maybe fifteen. I may be able to get them down to ten," he said.

I thought about the time, and wondered could they handle that if necessary. I didn't want them doing a day, though.

"Find a way to beat this case, I don't care if you gotta bribe Kimberly, do it," I said, walking out the door. I got down the steps and into the car. I started the ride up and noticed on the screen read "missed call."

"Missed call," I repeated to myself. I checked the number on the screen. It was a Baltimore number. It had to be Skills. How the fuck did he get the number to the car? I didn't even have the number. I pulled out my phone and called him back, then stepped out the ride. He picked up on the first ring.

"Yo, what up?" he said. He sounded like he was going through it.

"What up, nigga, I been trying to reach you for a couple of days," I said.

"Man, B, it's fucked up right now, it's all fucked up," he said.

"You a'ight?" I asked.

"Hell, naw, I ain't alright," he said.

"I need to holla at you about your situation out there," I said. I didn't want to say too much on the phone.

"I need you to come this way if you can. I really can't fly out right now," Skills said, looking down at his wounds. He was starting to bleed through his bandages.

Some shit must have kicked off there already. If I came there now, I probably would be in the middle of another war. I had to holla at Felix first, before I went out that way.

"Yeah, stay cool for about a day or two, and I'll be there," I said.

"A'ight," he said.

We hung up, and I called Felix after I got off the phone with him.

"Felix," I asked, as I heard someone pick up the phone.

"Yes, El Moreno," he said.

"Yeah, I need to talk to you," I said.

"Call me at this number." He gave me a number, then hung up. I called him right back.

"Let's talk," he said.

"This situation with our friend in Baltimore, how delicate is it?" I asked.

"Very, the men are allies to the Gulf Cartel," he said.

I thought about what I was about to say. "I can't let whatever going on, go down," I said, knowing that could cost me. If I went against the Cartels wishes, it could mean death. "I gotta help him out," I went on, sounding more like a plea. I knew I was skating on thin ice.

Felix was silent on the phone.

"I knew you wouldn't obey," he said. "You are a man that would protect his investment, even if it cost him his life." He paused for a moment. "I am one also, what do you need?"

I felt relieved at what he said. I thought I was about to be cut off.

"I need a crew," I said. I knew if I went to Baltimore, I would need a crew to deal with Arteaga.

"I will have you someone there, keep this between me and you, and you owe me," he said, then hung up.

* * *

"You play ball?" Geezy asked one of the other inmates that was coming out to the Rec. Yard.

"Naw," the guy said, walking past the court into the other room. Geezy started shooting the basketball alone. Tra and Freaky G were in other counties. He thought he was the only one in there that was on his case. Another block came out to Rec, and Boo walked out to the court. He saw Geezy playing basketball.

"You play?" Geezy asked.

"Yeah," Boo said, holding his hands up for the pass. Geezy passed him the ball. They started to play a game of twenty-one.

As they were playing Geezy asked Boo. "Where you from, homie?"

"I'm from the Lou, where you from?" Boo asked.

"I'm from Mt. Vernon," Geezy said. "I fucked around on the East Side, I knew some niggas over there but they fucked around in the Lou tough."

"Yeah," Boo said. He wasn't much for conversation. He didn't like to make friends like that. He couldn't trust 'em. "What you in here for?" Boo asked.

Geezy thought about that question and looked at Boo. It wasn't wise to tell another nigga your case, because they could hop on yo' shit and get some time off.

"Some bullshit," Geezy said. "What you in here fo'?"

"This bitch set a nigga up, she was fucking with some niggas from up yo' way."

"Yeah, I got hit by a bitch, too, a fam. What the bitch name that's on yo' case?" Geezy asked.

"Some bitch named Kimberly something," Boo said.

"Fuck, naw! That's the bitch that got me and my niggas," Geezy said. "You know a nigga name Rell from up yo' way?" he asked Boo.

Boo got tense at the mention of Rell. "How you know him, nigga?" he asked. He had a more serious look on his face.

Geezy noticed it.

"That's my nigga homie, straight up, you can ask 'em," Geezy said. "That bitch that set us up in this county, she right over in the female block."

Boo chopped it up with Geezy about the case and everything the feds was trying to trick them into doing. They'd never met, yet they were a part of the same conspiracy, all because of one person. They started to hear the guards calling others to go and see the nurse.

"Let's go to the nurse; we can holla at the bitches. They block right over by the nurse's office," Geezy said.

They hit the window and asked the guard could they see the nurse. The guard opened the Rec and let them out. He walked them around to the holding cell by the office and locked them inside. Soon as the guard left out the room, Geezy started to yell for the bitches.

"Hey," Geezy yelled. "Hey, girl, I know y'all hear me!"

It sounded like a white girl yelled back."Yeah, who is this, is this Mark?"

"Hell, naw! This ain't no Mark, bitch, where Kimberly at?" Geezy asked.

"Who?" the white girl asked.

"Kimberly, is a girl named Kimberly over there?" he asked.

"Yeah, hold on," she said.

They waited for a few minutes, then a guard came back in the room.

"Stop yelling or I'mma take you both to your cells," he said.

They just sat there in silence. They didn't want to say the wrong thing before they talked to Kimberly. The guard left again.

"Who is this?" a female yelled through the wall.

"You from St. Louis?" Geezy asked.

"Yeah, who is this?" she yelled.

Geezy looked at Boo.

"That's her right there," he said. Boo got up and walked over to the wall.

"Hey, that's why you wanted the money up front, so you can set a nigga up, huh?" Boo yelled.

"What?" she said. "Who is this?"

"You know who this is, I'm one of the dudes you set up, you met me in the Lou," Boo said.

She didn't respond. Boo knew she probably was over there fucked up about what she just heard.

"You know Rell?" she asked.

"Yeah, that's—" Boo stopped. He was about to say something he wasn't supposed to. "Yeah, that's my nigga."

"You be talking to him?" she said.

"Yeah," Boo lied.

"Tell him I was set up. That cop in Mt. Vernon put something in my car, he set me up."

"That's Smiley. She's talking about Smiley," Geezy said. "He be on that shit, too."

The guard came back into the room. "Okay. I told you to stop yelling at the girls, come on," he said. They walked back to the Rec.

"What block you in?" Boo asked.

"I'm in G, where you at?" Geezy asked.

"I'm in A, I'mma see if I could get over there. I'mma holla at you," Boo said as the guard continued to walk him back to his cell. He got in the block and called his lawyer. The lawyer said that he would be up to see him and Chad later on. He needed to talk to him about what she said, because if it was true, then she got set up by a crooked cop. Maybe they could beat the case.

* * *

We landed in Baltimore, and Skills picked us up. He was driving a rental car, and he had bandages on his arms and stomach.

"You alright?" Rell asked.

Skills explained what went on after he got back from seeing us. It seemed like he had something eles he wanted to say, but he was holding back.

"You owe dude some money or something?" I asked.

"Fuck, naw. I told you I squared him away on the first run," Skills said. "My man end up backstabbing me. He was on some fuck shit the whole time."

"Well, get up with Arteaga. Tonight, we will have a sit down with him," I said.

"What! A sit down?" Skills snapped. "Nigga, you can't sit down with this mafucka, what you gon' talk about?" he yelled.

"Nigga, calm the fuck down. We gon' sit down with him and see if we can discuss this little issue," I said.

Skills took a deep breath. "You taking this B. Pablo thing too far," he said.

Rell looked at him, then looked at me. I knew what was on his mind. Just knock Skills off and fuck it, fly on back to the crib since the nigga didn't want to roll with us. I wanted to help the nigga though, so I had him call Arteaga.

"I ain't gon' hit 'im up," Skills said.

"A'ight, I'll call him then," I said, calling Felix to get Arteaga's number.

Felix called back shortly with the contact.

"He's expecting your call," he said.

I hung up and called Arteaga.

"Yes, what do you want Pablo?" he laughed.

"I just want to talk to you, in person, and see if we can squash this situation," I said.

"Who do you think you are to want to sit at the table with me? I don't sit down with your kind," he said. I wanted to snap at that comment, but I held my temper.

"Believe me, I have friends like you do, and I can wreak the same havoc, so don't test me," I said.

He laughed at what I said. "Okay, Mr. Pablo, meet me at my restaurant tonight, around midnight." He hung up.

I called the guys that Felix got for me and let them know to meet me at the hotel in an hour. I hung up the phone.

"What he say?" Skills asked.

"Nigga, don't worry about what he said, just get ready to meet tonight," I said.

* * *

"I'm bout to go and get some more ice, you want something?" Shai asked Moni.

"Naw, I'm cool," Moni said. They were about to go out to get something to eat when they decided to stay in and order room service.

Shai got on the elevator. Someone ran and stuck their arm into the elevator door, causing it to open up again. Shai looked at the guy getting on. He was Puerto Rican, she could tell by the charm she saw in his slightly open shirt.

"How long you stay?" he asked. He had bad English. Shai looked back at him to see if it was anyone else he was talking to.

"Oh, not long," she said.

The elevator opened and Shai went to the vending machine. He followed behind her. He waved to two other dudes standing in the lobby area. Shai walked in the vending area and put her money in the machine.

Men entered the room with guns out.

"Don't say anything, or we will kill you," the one from the elevator said. "Where is Skills?"

"I don't know no Skills," Shai said.

"You fucking lying," he said. "Get her and take her to the car."

They walked Shai out to their truck and forced her inside. She didn't care anymore. She was just happy they didn't get Moni. She knew she could probably talk her way out of this. She probably wanted to fuck Skills up more than they did now.

Chapter Twenty-Six

Chad was escorted into the attorney visitors room. He sat down and took a deep breath. He was frustrated and tired of going through the emotions of facing a lot of time. Everyone in the county had been encouraging him to take a plea. They kept warning him about some 98% conviction rate the feds were supposde to have. Chad just told them, "I don't give a fuck bout a conviction rate." He was still taking it to trial.

The lawyer pulled out a stack of papers. "I got some bad news and some good news," he said, setting the papers on the table.

Chad didn't speak, he just looked on.

"Well, they're trying to charge a homicide from an overdose of heroin to the conspiracy. It seems someone by the name of Pacman, from Centralia, has stepped forth and cooperated with them on a guy by the name of Kill that's on the case,." The lawyer flipped through another stack of papers. "The good news is that all of that won't matter at all if I can subpoena some evidence from the cop car. Your cousin talked to Kimberly, and she admitted that the officer that arrested her planted drugs on the scene during a search. If I can prove that, we got'em. Everything after that would be inadmissible."

Chad felt a lot better now that there was something to go on. "IIow long you think it will take to find that out?" Chad asked. He was ready to get out of jail. He couldn't stand going from something to nothing.

"It shouldn't take long. The problem is if I can get into the police tation to obtain the video before it is destroyed. Ty and Rell told me to tell you both to not worry, they're doing the best they can," the lawyer said, closing the file.

* * *

The crew Felix sent down to Baltimore were just the type I needed. They was a group of eight young latinos. They looked like gang members. They each had a tattoo of a scorpion on their necks. They were armed already. We met them not too far from the restaurant. They pulled up in two black Yukons. We shook and greeted each other, then rode off to meet Arteaga. When we pulled up out front, Rell, Skills, and I got out to go in. The others stayed in the trucks.

"They ain't coming?" Skills asked.

"Naw. I ain't trying to show my hand this early, I'mma talk first," I said.

Rell stepped inside first, then me, then Skills. Skills stood behind me and whispered, "That's Tega in the black shirt."

Arteaga sat at a table near the back of the restaurant by himself. He had three other men sitting on each side of the table and one standing behind him. There was also one at the back door by the kitchen, and one at the door where we came in. There wasn't no telling how many mafuckas was in the back. Arteaga waved to us to come and sit.

Affiliated II

"Fifteen minutes is what I told Felix's guys to give us before they come in. Once it is up, duck," I whispered to Rell while walking over. I sat down on the opposite side of the table. Rell stood by me, and Skills sat at a table behind me.

I thought to myself how, not too long ago, I didn't like dealing with the politics of the game. Having sit downs and meetings, and for what? If a mafucka crossed the line, then fuck'em. That's how it was handled in the hoods across America. That's how we got it done. That's why we have so many on-going wars in the hoods also, because nobody wants to sit down and discuss the problems.

Chavez was right, there's no money in war. These sit downs were necessary, and I could see why now. It took the tension out of the game, as long as you got mafuckas who respect the game. Some mafuckas, you just don't have a choice.

"Arteaga," I said extending my hand.

"B. Pablo, is it the Black Pablo?" Arteaga grinned looking at his crew, and they laughed. "You got big balls, coming here. You came to my area and sold to my men," Arteaga said. "I own this, and you did not check with me for rent. That will cost you."

"Nothing is free right," I said with a fake grin. A year ago, I would have knocked his top back for tying to extort me. "I am a man who protects his investment, and you are trying to fuck up my investment. What would you do?" I asked.

Arteaga chuckled. "Look, Pablo or whatever you think you are, I don't know who gave you the balls to think you can sit with me and discuss what I do with my men." Arteaga looked at Skills. "I put you in this, and you prove no loyalty, not even enough to let me know." He cut a glance back at me. "I will sell him to you, since they call you Pablo. You can afford five hundred grand for him." When Arteaga said that, one of his men placed a gun to Rell's neck, then another snatched Skills out of his chair. "And five hundred for his bitch."

One of Arteaga's men came from out the back with Shai. I had my back to the door when they came out. Rell saw her first.

"Ty," Rell yelled.

I turned around and saw her, she stood there jerking trying to get away. She stopped when she noticed me and Rell. At the sight of Shai, I reacted on impulse. I reached for my gun and shot Arteaga in the head. Then I turned around to the gunman standing next to him and opened fire on them.

Rell followed my lead and started to shoot, too. Skills pushed the guy that was holding him and ducked.

I looked for Shai. She was on the floor. I didn't know if she was shot or not. I fired at the men moving in her direction. When I reached her, I felt a burn in my back and shoulder. I got hit twice. I rolled over to the floor. Shai immediately grabbed the gun and started shooting.

Felix's crew came in the door and helped to finish off the rest of Arteaga's men. Some of them tried running out the doors, but Felix's crew followed them and gunned them down. Skills ran out to the truck while Shai and Rell helped me to my feet.

They took me to a hospital, Rell hopped out and got help. They came out shortly with a stretcher, taking me in the emergency room. Shai and Rell hurried inside behind me. I was barely conscious. I had very short breaths, and I was drenched in blood.

Skills stood on, looking at me being wheeled in. He noticed two officers pointing their fingers at him and heading in his direction. He backed out of the door and got back in the truck and pulled off.

I laid there on the operating table. The slug in my back wasn't nothing to worry about. The one in my shoulder had struck a main artery. They clamped the artery and stopped the bleeding.

After a couple of hours I was okay to move around and talk.

When Shai walked in, I couldn't believe what I was seeing. I couldn't say anything. I thought she was just a vision at first. She hugged me tightly.

"Aww shit, baby," I said.

"Shut up," Shai said, holding her tears back.

I was still speechless and didn't know where to start.

"Moni?" I asked. I was scared of the answer, so I didn't want to ask the complete question.

"She's at the hotel, probably worried and wondering what's going on," Shai said.

"Do Rell know?" I asked.

"No," she said.

I got up and limped to put my clothes on. I kept the hospital shirt on until I was able to get another shirt, because they'd cut mine during the surgery.

The police in the hospital weren't worried about me at the time. They were still scrambling around looking for Skills. We crept out without a problem. We took a cab back to the hotel, where Shai knocked on the door to their room.

Moni stopped in mid-sentence when Rell stepped out from the side of the doorway. She hopped in his arms. "Nigga," she yelled, then kissed him.

Me and Shai walked in.

"We need to get out of here," I said.

Shai grabbed the little bags they had. She stepped up to me and handed me the watches.

"You was trying to get rid of me?" she asked.

I looked at the watches. "How you know I wasn't trying to send you a message?" I said.

"You ain't know, " she said.

"Naw, you right, I didn't know, but I'm glad I found out!"

* * *

On the plane home, we almost got flagged by security. My wounds were looking bad, and someone noticed it. We claimed a car accident while vacationing, and they bought it. The flight Marshal took down my information to run a check on it. The alias name came back clear, so he left us alone. I stared at Shai as she looked out the window.

We talked briefly about how Meno lied to both of us. Out of all the problems I went through, this one seemed the worst. As soon as Meno found out Shai and I were back together, there was no telling how he would react.

We made it to the apartment downtown. I got on the phone to schedule an emergency visit with a doctor, so that I could duck the hospital. I needed to get these wounds taken care of. I laid down on the bed. Shai came in the room and laid down beside me. She rubbed her hands gently over my wounds.

"How bad are you hurting?" she asked.

"Shit, I'm getting used to the pain now. I should make it as long as I can keep the bleeding down."

"What if I can make the blood rush to another spot?" She rubbed her hands down my pants.

"I know that ain't what the doctor ordered," I said, trying to get up.

She pushed me back down.

"I thought you was dead, and I went all this time alone. I'm tense and I need you." She leaned down and kiss me on the neck. "I'll be careful, I promise."

* * *

I checked my phone. The lawyer had been calling me, trying to get in contact. I called him back. "Yeah," I said when he got on the line. He was telling me he needed me to come in and meet him as soon as possible. "It'll be tomorrow, early in the morning," I said, then hung up.

"Who was that, the doctor?" Shai asked.

Without even realizing it, I hadn't told her about Chad and Boo situation. "Naw, that was the lawyer for Chad'n'em."

"Chad and who?" she said, lifting her head up.

Damn! I thought. "Yeah, Chad and Boo got set up, the feds got the case," I said.

"What they looking at?" she asked.

"Ten, maybe twenty," I said. I turned to her, biting my lip from the pain of moving around. "Look don't worry about it, I'm trying my best to beat the case."

Shai just turned over to the other side of the bed. I knew she was mad as hell. Probably not at me, but in general. The one thing she never wanted was them to get out there like that.

I woke up early and limped down the steps. I heard someone in the bathroom. I opened the door to find Moni bent over the toilet vomiting.

"You alright?" I asked, walking over to her aid.

"Yeah, just feeling sick," she said. Moni knew why she was vomiting. She was pregnant.

"You sure you alright?" I asked again.

"Yeah, yeah," she waved at me to go.

I closed the door. I knew that kind of sickness. That was a pregnancy sickness. I remembered it from Shai being pregnant. All I know is that it was no way it could be Rell's. I went down and grabbed my keys and went out to see the doctor.

Shai came down and found Moni in the kitchen preparing the meal. Moni wasn't looking too well.

"You alright?" Shai asked.

Moni tried not to answer the question. "You hungry?" she said.

"Moni," Shai yelled. Shai knew she was hiding something.

"Shai, I'm pregnant," Moni said.

Rell was about to enter the kitchen, but he overheard Moni. He stopped at the kitchen door, and tightened his fists. He walked in the kitchen.

"You what?" he said. He couldn't believe what she said. He looked back and forth at Moni and Shai. "You pregnant?" he asked.

"You don't understand," Moni said. She knew Rell was about to start assuming she was with another guy.

Shai felt she needed to say something, but she didn't know what to say. Moni never mentioned she was in a relationship with anyone.

"Rell, we thought—" Rell cut her off.

"Naw, fuck dat," he said. He was hurt, but he couldn't fault her completely. He had been out doing his thang also. But he didn't get anyone pregnant. He was about to turn around and leave out the kitchen. He stopped when Moni blurted out, "I was raped!"

"Story, he raped me," she cried.

Rell stopped and turned around. He looked at Shai, then at Moni,

"I'm sorry, I'm sorry," she cried.

Shai looked at Rell, he nodded for her to leave out the kitchen. He approached Moni and started to hug her. She had told him about Story and her cousin Kristy, but they didn't get a chance to complete the conversation. She had been afraid to tell him the entire situation.

"Naw, I'm sorry, I thought," he stopped and held her tight. The thought of someone raping her made him very angry, but it was nothing he could do now. Moni laid her head on his chest. Rell wondered now what she would do with the baby. They'd had a conversation about having a baby, when Shai was pregnant, and Moni had warned him that if he ever slipped up and got her pregnant, that they would have the baby. She didn't believe in abortions.

* * *

After the doctors visit, I stopped by the lawyer's office. He informed me of the evidence he needed to win the case. I knew that it would be a long shot for him to obtain it. It probably was lying in the trash somewhere. He said he had sent out subpoenas for the evidence. We only could hope that the detective hadn't already gotten rid of the tape.

* * *

Felix slammed down the phone. He had just talk to the Gulf Cartel. They informed him of Arteaga's death. He knew the Puerto Rican gangs would want bloodshed for Arteaga. They were looking for Pablo. Felix knew who Pablo was. The Puerto Ricans said they were aware of the presence of Mexicana when Arteaga was murdered, and they wanted Pablo or else. Felix couldn't go into another war, especially with the Puerto Ricans. He wondered should he give up El Moreno or should he try to keep El Moreno safe. Soon Felix would have to give them someone.

Chapter Twenty-Seven

Smiley walked into the station. The parking lot was swarming with I.A. detectives. Two men were walking out with boxes of tapes, each from the dates of the arrest. They had every video tape Kimberly was on. The money from the lawyer had given some influence to get Internal Affairs on the case. Smiley stopped one of the men.

"Hold on, what are you doing with the evidence?" he asked.

"It's new evidence now," the man said, walking away.

Smiley stormed into his boss's office.

"What the fuck is going on?" he yelled.

His boss looked up from signing some papers. "We got a subpoena to give up the traffic stop on Kimberly Barker, where is it? It's not logged in,"

"How the hell do I know, I logged it in," Smiley said.

"Look, I don't know who this woman is, but I.A.'s on the case. She's got some very powerful people behind her," he said, leaning back in his chair. "Now, I didn't see your signature on the sheet."

"What the fuck they want with the tape?" Smiley asked. Smiley saw one of the men coming out of his office. The tape was still in his drawer. He saw the desk drawer open. He usually kept it locked. The guy must have broken in it. He knew he should've gotten rid of the tape that night.

"Hey, hey," Smiley yelled at the guy. He bolted out of the office.

His boss was right behind him. He grabbed Smiley by the arm. "You better tell me what's on that tape," he hissed. "If you're hiding something I need to know."

Smiley looked around. "You know catching these bastards ain't easy as you think," he said. "Sometimes I gotta do what I gotta, play it their way."

"What's on the tape?" his boss asked.

"Nothing but me doing my fucking job," Smiley said, walking off.

* * *

"So when you gon' call him?" I asked Shai. I was ready to get this situation over with Meno. However it was going to play out, fuck it. I really hoped Shai would be able to convince him otherwise. If it came down to me making a choice, I choose her over the game any day. She put me in this shit.

"What happened with you that would make my father lie to me?" she asked.

I was quiet for a moment. I didn't know if I should tell her that I'd murdered El Chapo, or that the Cartels had granted me their favor, or that I was the first born to these connects. She might want to leave, in order to respect the Cartels rules. I never stood between her and Meno, and I didn't plan to now. So I decided to let her know everything.

Shai wasn't too happy to hear Meno being the new head of the Sinaloa. That would make him a permanent target to many others.

"How did you get close to El Chapo?"she asked.

"Felix, El Chapo's nephew," I said. "First, El Chapo wanted me to get rid of Felix, but come to find out, Felix was trying to stop the war and merge the Tijuana with the Sinaloa."

"Stop the war, merge the Cartels, who told you that?" she asked.

"Chavez. El Chapo found out he was with Felix and killed him, that's what set this shit into play."

"Chavez and Felix," she said aloud.

I could tell she was thinking about something, but what, I didn't know.

"No two Cartels will ever merge, the war will never stop," she said. "Felix," she whispered.

"You know him or something?"

"I met him before, in Chicago. Meno had me get something for him,"she said. "Felix had you kill El Chapo to secure his spot over the Sinaloa. He wants to merge the two into one. When I went to Chicago to take care of something for Meno, Felix and the Puerto Ricans had merged into a gang. Felix wanted to bring the Puerto Ricans business into our territories and start his own Cartel. But El Chapo and Meno did not want their business floating around. Felix got real pissed off, and that's when I overheard him say he would start his own Cartel, the Alacran, It means scorpion."

"Felix is the one who helped me with Arteaga," I said, I had doubts that Felix was trying to start his own Cartel.

"See, in the Cartels' eyes you're in their favor until you cross the line. Killing Arteaga was that line. Now the Cartels will order your death if they find out it was you," she said. "Felix set you up! When the time comes for him to take over, you will—" she stopped. She didn't want to say die. She didn't ever want to think of Ty dead again.

She made sense, but I didn't want to think I was a pawn in Felix's chess game. "Why didn't you ever say this to Meno?" I asked.

"I did. At the time, Felix was young, and they thought he was crazy, they didn't listen to me," she said. "We have to go to Meno."

We didn't pack anything at all. Shai called the airline and got tickets to Culiacan, where Meno had moved. He was excited to hear from Shai, but he didn't know that I would be coming with her.

I couldn't tell Rell about me and Shai going to see Meno and Felix. He would try and come along. So I lied and told him we were going to visit. If Shai was right about Felix, then he would try to wipe out the entire Sinaloa, even me. His influence amongst the other Cartel leaders was very strong, since it was him to implement the treaty. I had to find a way to gain some influence of my own.

* * *

Chad sat with the lawyer, watching the video of Smiley and Kimberly. The lawyer rewinded the tape several times, pointing to the screen with his pen.

"See, right there he is pulling something out of his pocket." The screen showed Smiley walking back to her car and opening the rear door. He then got out and opened the front passenger door. He open the console, and it was then when it looked clearly that he reached into a pocket of his, and pulled out the bag. "We got him."

Chad didn't say anything. He kept looking at the tape. He wanted to make sure. All the talk about the feds, and how they win most of their cases, gave him doubt about winning.

"I'm going to submit this to the judge and file a motion to suppress the evidence. Most likely we will get it. The only thing is, after this, you both better not even be caught with paraphernalia, because they will be on your every move."

Chad shook his hand and headed back to the block. He smiled as the door closed. He knew that would be the last time they closed a door on him like that again.

* * *

Pulling up to Meno's, I thought about how I would talk Meno into getting the heads over to the house. I had completely forgotten about the me and Shai situation until she told me that she would do the talking.

Juarez saw me walk in with Shai and gave me a smirk. He had the "that's all on you look." When we entered the kitchen, Meno was eating. He smiled when he saw Shai, and got up out of his chair to hug and kiss her. When he saw me, he went into a deadly stare. He kept a stern look on his face as he looked at Shai, then at me.

"So, you both found out," he said, sitting back down.

Shai sat down beside him. "Why did you lie to me?" she asked.

"You know how the business is run, no family. You are my family, not his! I will do everything to protect you!" He got up from the table and rushed at me, but Shai stood up in between us.

225

"And you," he looked at me coldly. "You did not listen, don't mix family with business."

I knew Meno wanted to kill me, but he wouldn't while Shai was here. "You love my Shai that much?" he asked.

"Yeah, that much," I said. He meant that I would risk dying.

"Then we do business no more, neither you do business with anyone else," he yelled,."It's over!" He sat back down.

I sat down, and Shai looked at me. She was shocked at my answer. I was giving up the game for her.

"I must get ready, I must meet with the Gulf and Juarez in a minute," Meno said, getting up from the table. I knew this was my time to explain.

I stood up; the pain from the wounds were starting to hurt again. Meno saw that I was wounded.

"Before you go, can we talk?" I asked. After I explained the situation with me and Skills to Meno. He told me the Gulf Cartel wanted this meeting, because they suspected something with Felix, and to find out who Pablo was. It seemed to them that Felix was the only person who actually knew who he was. I had to tell Meno everything, I couldn't leave him out in the cold.

"Felix gave me the men to go at Arteaga," I said to Meno.

Meno figured out Felix's plan as well. He glanced at Shai. He remembered her telling him about this years ago. He didn't think Felix would rise this far, let alone above his uncle.

The Gulf and Juarez Cartels were coming in. Each came with several guards. Meno greeted them and offered them drinks.

"Gentlemen, so nice to see you again," Meno said. "It seems another problem has emerged." He looked at Sanchez, head of the Gulf. "It also seems we are being fooled into a trap."

Their expressions grew serious.

"Our friend Felix," Meno said, "has plotted to form his very own Cartel, the Alacran."

One of the guards moved to cover up the scorpion tattoo on his neck.

"We cannot let this happen," Meno added.

"How do you know of this?" the Gulf spoke out.

"Our friend El Moreno, he was responsible for the death of Arteaga, but only through the hands of Felix. It was Felix's men there with him." Meno looked up at the sound of tires screeching. He saw Felix coming in the house with two carloads of armed men. Meno looked back at the leaders, then looked at the door.

Meno hurried and sat down, and I sat with him. Felix burst into the room looking around in all directions. His men came in behind him. "Was there an early meeting I don't know about?" he said, looking at Meno.

"The meeting is tonight, me and Ty was here discussing business. What are you doing here?" Meno asked.

"Business, I just dropped by," Felix said, sitting down next to me. I looked and noticed a scorpion tattoo on his neck, the same as the one the men had in Baltimore.

"El Moreno, or B. Pablo, you're a man with many aliases," Felix said, tapping me on the back.

Meno passed me a glance. He wanted me to challenge Felix.

"You're a man of many aliases also, Alacran," I said.

Felix looked up from cutting his cigar. His guards moved at the comment I made. Felix waved his hand in the air stopping them.

One of Felix's men that was posing as a guard for the Gulf came out with the other leaders at gunpoint. They pushed Sanchez and the Juarez brothers into the room. "They were in there listening, boss," he said.

Felix walked over to Sanchez.

"You plan this, you will never—uh." The feeling of the sharp blade penetrating his stomach cut Sanchez off.

Felix pulled the blade out and Sanchez fell to the floor.

"Yes, I planned this," Felix said. He turned around to Meno.

Meno had a collection of rare blades over the mantle, and Felix grabbed one. "You know I wanted you to become part of this El Moreno, but hey, you can't always have what you want." He laughed. I saw Shai and Juarez standing at the crack of the door. Juarez looked wounded. Shai was reading the room, trying to see how many men were in there. When she saw Felix in sight with the blade facing Meno, she pushed in the door and started shooting. I grabbed Meno and ducked for cover behind the desk.

Meno opened the drawer and grabbed a couple of guns he had stashed. I hopped up and dropped one of the guards. The Juarez brothers saw this as their opportunity and started to shoot also. The guards were trapped in the corner of the room. We were shooting at them from all sides. I got up and finished off the remaining guards. I stepped over Felix where he lay clenching his side. Shai had hit him when she opened fire on the room. I saw the blade on the side of him. I reached down and picked up the blade, lifted it.

"In memory of El Chapo." Then I dropped the blade.

Shai rocked back and forth, holding Meno in her arms. Her face was flooded with tears. Meno was hit in his upper body several times. He was still breathing. I was bleeding, too. The wounds had opened back up during the shooting.

Affiliated II

The Juarez brothers helped with Meno. They rushed him to a private doctor, someone that Meno knew personally. Shai laid in the room after the doctor did his work. Meno was in stable condition now. The doctor stitched and bandaged me and Juarez, too. He said Meno would need to rest for a day or two, then he would be better.

I called home to see if Rell and Moni was okay. After I got off the phone with him, Shai came into the room. She looked exhausted. I could tell this was taking a toll on her. I didn't want her to hurt like that at all.

"He'll be alright, don't worry," I said hugging her. She rested her head on my chest.

"You really gon' give it all up for me?" she asked.

"Naw, I really gave it all up for you. It's over, and it better be worth it," I said.

She smiled, that's all I wanted to see.

Chapter Twenty-Eight

"Where Moni and Rell?" Shai asked. "We gon' miss Chad's and Boo's court date!" Shai thought we were on our way to see Chad and Boo at court. Rell had already told me the lawyer got the case dropped by suppressing the evidence. That sparked a lot of other cases getting overturned, due to Smiley. Chad and Boo was with them in the truck when they pulled up. Moni smiled as she got out.

"What the hell you smiling for, y'all late. We been out here for damn near a hour," Shai yelled.

Chad and Boo got out, looking rough. Both of them needed a haircut and trim.

"What up, cuz," they yelled, pulling up their pants. Shai saw them and yelled.

"Ooh shit," she said. "When y'all get out?" Shai hugged them and gave them a kiss like she was they mama.

"What the fuck," Chad said moving his face.

"We just left the court house. The feds was mad as fuck," Boo said. We got inside the truck and pulled off. "Man, let's go get something to eat, I'm hungry as shit!"

"Hell, yeah, all that bullshit food, I ain't ate in hellas!" Chad said.

I looked at Rell. "It's over with, homie," I said.

Rell looked at me with a smirk. He looked back to make sure Shai couldn't hear him.

"Yeah right, nigga, I know better."

* * *

"C.O.! C.O.," Skills yelled down the hallway through the food slot on the door. He had been beating on the door all day. They'd caught him trying to get off the hospital lot. He had been in segregation for a couple of days. The Puerto Ricans in the county had a hit out on him. They'd attempted to kill him twice already. He knew he wasn't safe there. He had to find a way to get out.

"What the fuck is it now, Moore?" A tall, fat county guard asked, walking up and hitting the door with his flashlight.

"I need to talk to somebody," Skills said.

"You talked to somebody already, who you need to talk to now?" the guard said.

"Naw, you don't understand, I ain't safe here. I need to talk to somebody, I gotta get out of here," Skills said. "I'll tell em whatever they want to know."

* * *

Rell and Moni walked out of the Abortion Clinic, in Granite City, IL. Moni had her head down as she walked to the ride. Rell just looked on, he didn't know what to say. He couldn't figure out the right words to comfort her. They got in and drove off.

"You hungry, or what?" Rell asked.

Moni just looked at him.

"What?" Rell said. He didn't know if she was about to snap or not.

"I just had an abortion, why would I be hungry? I'm sleepy, and tired," she said. "Take me home!"

"You alright, though?" Rell asked.

"Yeah, I'm okay. You know I wasn't gon' have the baby. I probably wouldn't have treated the baby right. I had to do it."

"So, you cool now, right? I can start going bareback now? You'll have an abortion?" Rell swerved and almost went off the rode when Moni reached over and slapped him twice, trying to hit him in the face.

"Nigga! If you get me pregnant, we having it, ain't no abortions with you. And I want one now, so you might as well get ready!"

THE END

www.ingramcontent.com/pod-product-compliance
Lightning Source LLC
Chambersburg PA
CBHW060317260626
47160CB00007B/2647

* 9 7 8 0 6 9 2 4 2 6 8 5 2 *